WEARING SKIN

12 HORROR SHORT STORIES

SIMON PAUL WOODWARD

CONTENTS

THE ANGEL OF LOUGHBOROUGH JUNCTION

Alex pulled his jacket tight around him and sat down on a backless wooden bench. Stan adjusted his woolly hat so it covered his ears and sat down alongside his friend.

"It's cold," said Stan.

"It's not hot," said Alex.

They looked at the big townhouse on the opposite side of Cold Harbour Lane. Perforated green metal covers fitted snug to the bricks, protecting its windows and front door. They'd watched it on and off for a week and had seen no sign of owners, tenants or squatters.

"All roads lead to Loughborough Junction," said Stan.

"So it seems," said Alex.

"Shall we?"

Alex wiped his runny nose with a sleeve.

"Why not," he said.

They crossed the road and entered an alleyway that ran along the side of the house. Draping folded coats over glass shards set in concrete, they clambered over the wall and dropped into an unkempt garden. More metal grilles sealed the windows, but a close inspection revealed a triangular corner levered upwards where somebody had tried, but failed, to break in.

"Crowbar job," said Stan as he examined the window.

"I bow to your superior expertise," said Alex.

Stan waggled his arm and a crowbar that had been hidden up his sleeve slid into his fist. He bent to lever the cover free. Alex sat on a low wall and looked up at the first floor. He pulled a carton of milk from a jacket pocket and opened it. Stan grunted as he worked at the window. Alex downed half of the milk and offered the other half to his friend. Stan shook his head, spraying sweat.

Alex nodded at the house, showing his respect. Only top-notch security could work Stan into such a fluster.

At present they were living in a tower-block squat just off the Camberwell New Road, but the group politics (and *politics* politics) of the flat had become increasingly sour. As the newest arrivals, it had fallen upon them to find fresh digs. Anyway, another move would further confuse the trail they had worked so hard to hide, and further confuse the Institution.

There was a metallic wrenching sound followed by the squeak of wood, and the cover clanged to the floor. Stan punched out the window with the crowbar. Alex applauded softly. Stan took a theatrical bow.

"Shall we?" said Stan, sweeping a hand towards the open window.

"After you," said Alex.

"No! After you," said Stan.

As soon as they climbed through the window, they saw that they had struck lucky. The house was in excellent condition, full of furniture and appliances, but had been unoccupied for years. A deep layer of dust covered every-thing. Old cobwebs hung like dreadlocks in every corner. A flick of a light switch revealed the miracle of connected electricity. Stan smiled at the landslide of mail that swept down from the front-door letterbox. He'd have fun sorting through that.

In the kitchen they found the remains of a meal for four. Half-empty plates covered in fuzzy mold. Dregs of wine had turned to granular purple stains. Burnt-out candles. Upstairs, the beds were a hastily-left tangle of sheets. There were men's and women's clothes in the drawers and wardrobes.

"Aladdin's cave," said Alex, opening a bedside table and scooping out necklaces twisted into a glittering knot.

A heavy thump sounded on the ceiling above them and they both looked up.

"Pigeons?" said Alex.

"Maybe," said Stan.

"Big pigeons?"

"Possible."

HOLLYWOOD LOVED MARTIN LAVENDER. Within four years of arriving, he had mutated from unknown Euro-trash to Player status. He was this month's Messiah. The media lionised him as the hyper-hyphenate: actor-screen-writer-director-producer-businessman-instigator of public debate. Now he had a secret addition to his list of achievements – double murderer.

"Kensington, Mr Lavender?" said his driver.

Martin hesitated. For a moment he toyed with the idea of visiting the house in Loughborough Junction, but it wasn't time yet. When Madeleine was dead, he would visit the house.

"Kensington," he said.

The driver eased the Rolls Royce into the flow of traffic – other motorists deferring to its majesty – and headed away from the airport towards the city.

Martin slipped a hand inside his jacket and squeezed the leather case in the inside pocket. Everything was okay. They were still there. He did this at least a hundred times a day, but the relief obtained by feeling the case never lasted more than a few minutes. He was soon itching to reassure himself again.

He closed his eyes. They felt gritty, sore, overworked. Exhaustion, physical and emotional, had a vice-like grip on him. It had been profoundly painful for him to murder Tom and Alyson. It had wounded his soul, but it had been necessary. It was him or them. Now, it was nearly over. Only Madeleine remained. With the resources at Martin's disposal, she couldn't hide forever.

He fell asleep, waking an hour later, eyes watering. He looked around, disorientated, as the car rolled into the garage below a row of grand Victorian townhouses. Martin owned the entire block and lived in the penthouse. He'd restricted access to his penthouse to a single lift guarded by one of his security team.

Inside, he relished the silence of the flat. He pulled the case from his suit pocket and locked it in the wall safe. He filled a bath and lay in it for half an hour, occasionally running a little more hot water. The steam always soothed his eyes. Afterwards, he pulled on a robe, fixed himself a glass of single malt and padded around the apartment, flicking through film scripts.

He noticed a pulsing red light on his answerphone. Only half a dozen of his closest associates had this number. He pressed the play button. It was probably Henderson, his

American partner who lived with a phone attached to one ear.

The beeps sounded and Madeleine spoke.

"Tom was your best friend," she said. The message ended.

How had she found this number? Had she followed him back to England? He slammed a fist into the machine, its plastic crunching, blood welling from his knuckles.

"Shit," he said, wrapping a handkerchief around his hand.

WHEN THEY LOCATED the attic stairway, Stan indicated that, by virtue of his height and bulk, Alex had earned the right to be the leader of this particular expedition. Alex thanked him with an ironic bow.

Another heavy thump sounded through the house as they reached the attic door.

"One small step for squatter kind," said Stan.

Alex grinned, counted to three and pushed open the door. The attic was large and gloomy and at first glance appeared to be empty. As their eyes became accustomed to the dark, they saw a shape at floor level in the centre of the room. They each took a step inside. Stan patted the wall on the right of the door, found a light switch and flipped it on. A single, shade-less bulb stuttered into life.

"Jesus Christ," said Stan.

"And his father," added Alex.

The creature in the middle of the room erupted into a frenzy of thrashing movement, smacking its huge wings against the floor. Clouds of dust filled the space and the light bulb swung wildly on its length of flex.

Stan and Alex coughed, rubbing dust particles from their smarting eyes. Eventually, the creature seemed to tire of its wild movements and lay still, panting.

It was magnificent, and at least eight feet tall. It was facing away from them, its face covered by long silver-white hair. It was human in form, except for the marvellous wings that grew from its shoulders, which would easily reach from wall to wall if outstretched. A faint iridescence pulsed through its plumage.

"You came back," it said in a musical voice.

Alex and Stan exchanged glances.

"I don't think we've been here before," said Stan.

"I'm sure we haven't," said Alex.

The creature paused and shifted its position slightly. Its musculature tightened.

"Who are you? Did *they* send you?" it asked.

"We're nobody," said Stan.

"And we certainly weren't sent by *them*," said Alex.

"We don't normally get on with *them*."

"We're not *their* cup of tea."

The creature released a long sigh and, with a great effort, lifted itself on one wing and flopped over onto its back. It lay panting, exposing a voluptuous hermaphrodite body that was naked save for dust, cuts and enormous indigo bruises. Its eye sockets were an empty ragged mess, its face marred by a mask of dried blood and mucus. Despite this cruel disfigurement, it was still breathtakingly beautiful; its face longer and thinner than a human's, its skin stretched tight, virtually transparent but luminous.

"Do you see the markings painted around the perimeter of the room?" said the creature.

Stan and Alex had to squat down to see the faded blue symbols.

"Yes," they said in unison.

"They hold me captive. The thieves who took my eyes wove them."

"They don't sound like model citizens," said Stan.

"They planned to use my eyes to raise themselves up amongst men."

Stan bent down towards the creature. "Shall I clear away the markings?" he said.

"I can only leave the markings as I entered; complete."

"How can we help you?" said Alex.

"Anything," said Stan.

"Return to me what was stolen. I will reward you handsomely."

"It's as good as done," said Alex.

"We're on the case," said Stan.

"The leader's name is Lavender. He has the blackest heart. If he is not dead, he will be infamous. Search him out."

The creature raised one of its wings towards them.

"Pull free a feather," it said.

Alex grasped a feather and felt a tingling pulse travel up his arm. As he pulled it free from the creature's wing, it transformed into a thick roll of fifty-pound notes.

"To ease your quest," sighed the creature, sounding exhausted by their conversation.

Alex turned to leave, but Stan had a last question for the creature.

"Are you an angel?"

"To some," it replied.

"You're not Gabriel, are you?"

The creature laughed. The sound was like a narcotic and made their heads spin. Blood hummed around their bodies. "Most call me Dubious."

"The Angel Dubious," said Stan, "I like that.

THE SOHO STREET below Martin's window bustled with its usual energy, but there was still no sign of his meeting – this supposed wonderkid, Jaz Winstanley. He was two hours late. Martin could wait. It heightened the anticipation.

He'd decided that he wanted to make *the* great British movie. He'd already conquered Hollywood, and now he would do the same to Blighty. He'd always had it in his mind to make the move back one day, and the double-murder investigation dominating the network news bulletins had hastened the move.

He was eager to work again, to sweep away any residual guilt about Tom and Alyson with a torrent of creativity. But his people had experienced problems securing the rights to a novel that was the perfect vehicle for what he wanted to do. The twenty-four-year-old author Jaz Winstanley had decided that Martin Lavender was not the director-producer-writer-human being he'd want to transfer his satirical *magnum opus* to the silver screen. Martin was too Hollywood. Too vulgar.

Using tried and tested methods, Martin had tested Winstanley's vulgarity threshold. His agent had turned down an offer of two hundred thousand pounds flat, then five hundred thousand, finally sweating his way to two million before agreeing to even meet with Martin to discuss *the possibility of a deal.*

That was all he needed – a one to one. Once he had Winstanley in the office, he'd really be able to *see* him, and then they would get down to some real bargaining. He felt a thrill of anticipation as he thought of the sweet revelations that the glasses would grant him. How gratifying it would be to know exactly what the jumped-up little wanker was thinking; to send him squirming down blind alleys, build up his hopes, crush them at the most crucial moments. He didn't doubt for a second that the rights would be his by the end of the day.

He treated himself to an appetiser before Winstanley arrived. The case was in his suit pocket. He pulled it out and removed the spectacles. In the sunlight, the smaller lenses set within the main ones were visible to the naked eye. Rainbow colours moved across them like oil on water.

He hadn't thought about *the night* for a long time, and he did not understand what made him conjure up the image now. The four of them standing in the candlelit attic, chanting, sweating, painting the symbols around the room's perimeter. Blood spots on the floor as he slit his arm. Madeleine's fearful face. The unexpected mirrors that appeared around them – reflections going on forever. The angel falling through the mirrors and smashing against the floor. Their collective shock overcome, pumping anaesthetics into the creature. Its otherworldly moan, almost like wind chimes. The scalpel removing its eyes, then slicing them open, shaking fingers rooting for the lenses in a mess of tissue and vitreous fluid. Running from the room, laughing like children. The four of them hugging and kissing and gasping with relief.

They should never have plotted against him.

Martin filed away the memory.

He slipped on the glasses and looked down at the street. As he focused on pedestrians, images flashed into his mind. He didn't bother to linger; he was only browsing, distracting himself. Ponytail, black suit, tortoise-shell glasses shuffling along, terrified of an interview, super-imposing his girlfriend into the position of a Torquemada-like interviewer. Jeans, checked shirt and hangover, worried about the outcome of an evening football match, a horse race, scared he might see somebody from work, he'd called in sick. An achingly cool couple, woman thinking of her female lover, man searching his memory for shared experiences that they could discuss. Two youthful men, one tall, one short, wearing identical black suits. They looked up at his window, but there were no images. Martin concentrated on them and a painful, blinding brightness filled his eyes.

He closed his eyes and snatched the glasses from his face. His head hummed with hangover intensity. That had never happened before. Gingerly, he opened his eyes; flecks of light danced across his retinas. He felt as if he had mistakenly looked into an arc light. He peered out of the window. The men in suits were no longer there. *It must have been sunlight on the shop window*, he told himself, as he rubbed his temples.

The intercom buzzed and Vicky, his receptionist, told him that Jaz Winstanley had arrived. Martin told her to send the author up to his office. As an afterthought, he asked her to call in one of his bodyguards.

VICKY LOOKED up from the screen of her MacBook Pro when she heard the door open. She put on her best glossy-lipped welcome smile.

"Good morning. How can I help you?" she said to the two identically-dressed young men who stepped confidently into the reception room.

They looked at each other and smiled. *Fifty quid says*

they're annoying ex-art students on the blag for work, she thought, and smiled even more brightly.

"We have an appointment with Mr Lavender," said the taller of the two.

"1.30pm," added his companion.

"Well, I'm afraid Mr Lavender is already in a meeting at the moment and it's scheduled to last the rest of the day. I don't think he has anything else in his diary for today."

Vicky made a quiet tutting noise as she pretended to scrutinize the diary. "No, nothing. Are you sure that your appointment was for today?" she asked.

"Quite sure," said Mr Tall.

"I believe we arranged the appointment through your good self," said Mr Short with a sincere grin.

"Oh, I don't think so. I've got an excellent head for times and names and that sort of thing. It's my job, you see. Could you give me your names, please?"

No names were forthcoming. They just looked at each other with idiotic grins.

"If you give me your names, I'll see if I can pencil in a meeting with Mr Lavender," she said. "Possibly next month."

Mr Short reached into a jacket pocket and pulled out a thick roll of fifty-pound notes. He peeled notes from the bundle. One by one, he laid them on her desk.

"Our problem is," said Mr Tall, "we need to see Mr Lavender urgently. I suppose you could say that it is a matter of life and death."

"Can you help us?" said Mr Short.

Vicky's first instinct had been to yell at them to get out of the room, but now she wasn't so sure. The pile of notes became thicker; there must have been two thousand pounds sitting on the desk, at least, and the bundle of notes in Mr Short's hand looked the same size.

"Can you help us?" asked one of the men. She wasn't sure which. Her attention was focused on the growing mound of notes.

"Well..."

"We would be ever so grateful."

"I suppose I could..."

The door to the street opened ushering in the sound of traffic before she could finish her sentence. With an impressive effort, she raised her eyes from the money. It was Paulo, one of Martin's bodyguards. She vaguely remembered calling him on his mobile a few minutes ago.

"Do we have a problem here, Vic?" he asked.

"Er... no. I don't think so," she said, shaking her head clear and looking at Tall and Short. What had they been saying to her?

"Well, we really must make a move," said Mr Tall.

"We have to do lunch," expanded Mr Short, with a world-weary shake of his head and a shrug of his shoulders.

Before she could say a word, they nodded politely to Paulo and walked out of the reception. As the door clicked shut, she remembered the money. She dropped her gaze to her desk, but it was empty. Shit! Where had it gone?

"Are you okay?" asked Paulo as Vicky dropped to her stockinged knees and rooted around under her desk.

THE PRAWNS HAD BEEN PASSABLE. The lobster, as always, superb. Martin drained his glass of Chablis and smiled at the actress sitting on the opposite side of the table.

Lucy Minto was angling for a major role in his new

project. The news that Jaz Winstanley had sold the rights of his novel to Martin had spread through the film community within hours. The day after they had signed the deal, Lucy's agent had been wheedling away down the phone, trying to set up a meeting. Martin had fended him off for a week before he caved in and consented to a one-to-one lunch with the pulchritudinous starlet. He didn't want to rush things.

For seven days he savoured his mental rape of Winstanley and encouraged his cohorts to greater exertions in their search for Madeleine. She was still at large, leaving messages on his mobile, threatening to go to the press. As ludicrous as her story would sound, he couldn't risk hacks snooping around the house in Loughborough Junction.

Winstanley had been much easier to deal with. As soon as he twitched his way into the office, Martin knew that he was a bag of neurosis and inadequacy. He didn't even need the glasses to see that. But when he placed those magical lenses before his eyes, what secrets he found! What knots of guilt and confusion! A sex addict, a cocaine addict, a potential suicide risk (excellent, if timed to coincide with the release of the film), a lonely child and a lonely adult. He hadn't written a word since the completion of his first novel and the idea terrified him he was written out; that it was all over, just as it had begun. A one-novel wonder hoovering up coke, destroying every one of his relationships through insecurity and infidelity, huddling around the warmth of adulation that barely reached his frozen core.

Martin had rummaged through Winstanley's mind with glee, prodding a pressure point here, twisting a phobia there, tugging out the twisted mess of his mind and holding it like an x-ray image to the light. He was a demented surgeon of dreams. Winstanley signed the contract with tears in his eyes. Martin shook his hand and promised him a wonderful partnership.

Lucy was saying something to him about Buddha, gesturing with the flat of her hand. Martin drifted from his reverie and focused on the actress' pout. He wondered whether her lips were collagen enhanced. In a few minutes, he would find out. He would slip on the glasses and push into her yielding mind; standard procedure for all his informal auditions.

Martin nodded at what she was saying and hummed his agreement. His attention had been pulled elsewhere. Paulo, sitting at a table by the entrance to the restaurant, was talking animatedly into his phone. A grin spread across the bodyguard's face. He looked towards Martin, judging whether it would be prudent to interrupt his employer. Martin waved him over. He had a tingling feeling inside. He could guess the news, but he wanted to hear Paulo say it.

"They've found her," he whispered directly into Martin's ear.

MARTIN ONLY HAD to wait fifteen minutes before Madeleine emerged from a doorway at the bottom of the tower block. Even swaddled in a thick jumper, he could see that she had lost weight and vitality. A life on the run had not suited her. All her dreams had been of idle luxury. Martin crushed a worm of guilt that had the audacity to rear its head. She was the one who should feel guilty. She'd betrayed him. Conspired with Tom and Alyson to steal the angel's eyes. They were his. He had summoned the creature, bled for it, and performed the surgery.

Madeleine crossed the road and entered a vandalised phone box. She dialled a number, spoke briefly into the receiver and then slammed it down. She exited and scuttled back across the road, all the time glancing up as if she feared an attack from above.

Martin slipped from the car and followed at a discreet distance. He touched the knife in his pocket and then put on the glasses. He had to look into her mind one last time. Instantly, he realised he'd made a mistake. Her interior was a maelstrom of rage. Fever dreams. Waking nightmares. Pitch darkness formed from hatred, his image at the centre, leather-winged harpies swooping to slash and maul, suffocating anger. He yanked off the glasses and heaved prawns and lobster onto the pavement.

Any semblance of guilt had now been obliterated. She'd fallen prey to madness. He had to finish it now.

Inside the tower block, the lift was out of order. He could hear her steps echoing up the stinking stairwell. He removed his shoes and padded after her, careful to avoid glass and urine.

They climbed ten floors, Martin always one floor behind, just out of sight. Then Madeleine's footsteps stopped. Martin stood still, breathing as quietly as possible, listening for any sign of her position.

She must have gone into a flat, he thought. Quietly, he tiptoed to the top of the stairs and peered onto the landing. There was no sign of life. One flickering light cast twitchy shadows upon the four doors that faced each other. Nothing else. He stepped onto the landing, his gaze shifting from doorway to doorway. Ears screaming in the silence.

"Martin?" said a voice behind him.

He turned around. Madeleine was sitting in the shadows on the stairs leading to the eleventh floor. She moved into the flickering light, exposing her ravaged face and a gun pointing at Martin.

"Martin," she said. Her smile was like a bullet.

"Wait," said Martin, raising his hands, palms towards her.

"What do you see now?" she asked, squeezing the trigger.

Martin closed his eyes before the shot exploded into the confined space. Bangs echoed up and down the stairwell. He tensed his body and waited for the searing pain he imagined would result from a bullet wound.

Nothing happened.

No pain.

"Unfortunate," said a male voice.

"But unavoidable," added another voice.

Martin opened his eyes. Two men wearing identical suits stood before him. The shorter of the two was looking him in the eyes and pointing a gun in his face. The taller of the two was pointing another gun at Madeleine, who lay curled and still on the stairs. Blood clotted the front of her jumper.

"Mr Lavender has caused a good deal of trouble," said the tall man, turning to face Martin.

"An awful amount of trouble."

"I can..." said Martin, halting as the taller man held up a cautionary finger. Gently, he reached inside Martin's jacket and pulled out the glasses case. He slipped them into his own inside pocket.

Martin could barely contain himself. A moan escaped his lips and his muscles twitched with suppressed violence; how dare they? They may as well have cut out his heart. Suddenly, he realised that he had seen these two before, standing on the pavement opposite his office – the flash of light. He hadn't been able to see them with the glasses.

"Who are you?" he asked.

"Repo men," said Alex, just before he smacked the butt of his pistol against the side of Martin's head. The hyper-hyphenate slumped to the floor.

"Too hard?" asked Alex.

"No, just right," said Stan.

MARTIN'S FACE WAS AGONY. He tried to open his eyes, but the light from the bulb was too much for the delicate state of his head. The light on the landing hadn't been that bright. Where was he? Where were Tall and Short?

Slowly, he opened his eyes to a slit. The light and pain in his head caused tears to well up and spill down his cheeks. He wiped them away and opened his eyes wider. Tears blurred his vision. He blinked them away and saw the attic, the Angel Dubious sitting cross-legged before him. Out of the corner of his eyes, he saw Tall and Short sitting on chairs, guns resting on their laps.

The glasses were on the floor between him and Dubious, slick rainbows gliding across the inner lenses. The angel's mutilated face was impassive.

Martin weighed up his limited options: If he made a break for the door, the suits would shoot him; if he did nothing, Dubious would be free to take its revenge. There was only one option: he had to talk his way out, bargain with the angel. Martin glanced down at the glasses. One glimpse inside that celestial head was all he needed.

"Welcome home," said Dubious.

It took Martin a beat to recover from the beauty of its voice. He gathered his wits and made his play.

"I'm glad to see you looked after the place," he said, shifting dust on the floor with one hand, coughing.

"I've not felt well disposed towards household chores."

"Come now, surely a rest does us all good now and then."

Martin inched forward. Slid his hand towards the glasses.

"Are the others dead?" asked the angel.

"They became greedy."

"And threatened your model of restraint."

"Now, now," said Martin, laughing. "Sarcasm doesn't suit immortals."

He was sure that the angel couldn't see him or sense his movements. The two suits were immobile on their chairs. The glasses were only a foot away.

"Did you achieve anything?" asked the angel.

"Lots of things."

"Anything I should congratulate you on?"

"Well... let me think for a minute."

ALEX AND STAN watched Martin mumble nonsense and edge towards the glasses. He flashed a glance at them. As instructed by Dubious, they did nothing - even when Martin lanced out an arm, grabbed the glasses and pushed them onto his face, a triumphant grin splitting his skin. They sat still, watched him back up against the wall and gaze at the angel. His expression slid from joy into panic, terror and, finally, vacuity. The colours within the lenses pulsed and swirled. Martin moaned and his mouth dropped open. Drool slid onto his chest. His body convulsed, and he slipped to the floor, lying on his side as little curls of smoke rose from behind the rainbow lenses.

Dubious laughed as it reached out and retrieved the spectacles. Martin's eye sockets were burnt, black and empty. A wisp of smoke escaped his mouth. Dubious arched its back and spread its wings as it put on the glasses. Dust and dirt fell from its body. Its wings shimmered. It removed the glasses, now just frames, and looked at Alex and Stan through golden irises. It bowed low to them.

Alex and Stan nodded humbly in reply.

With a sweep of its magnificent wings, Dubious coated the floor, ceiling and each wall with mirrors. In every direction, black-suited figures and a slumped dead body reflected into infinity. There was only one Dubious; none of the surfaces could catch its image.

The angel pulled two feathers from its body and handed one each to Alex and Stan.

"I trust you will use them wisely," it said.

Without waiting for an answer, the angel folded its wings against its back and walked through one of the mirrors. Immediately, all of the other mirrors evaporated.

"All roads lead to Loughborough Junction," said Alex.

"So it seems," said Stan.

"Shall we go?"

"Why not?"

MANNY AND THE MONKEYS

The night before he finally finished the novel, Manny dreamt of the monkeys again. Thousands of monkeys surrounding his isolated house, capering across the roof, swinging from guttering, gibbering and screeching, grinning through the windows. He woke when one of them rang the old ship's bell on the porch.

Fatigued but excited, he hurried to his study and began to write. So intense was his focus on the words filling the screen, sunlight and shadow moved with time-lapse speed across his study. And, at last, it was done. He typed the final two words with seven exaggerated stabs of a forefinger: *The End*. He always did it this way.

He saved the file and then backed it up half a dozen times. A tear of relief squeezed from his eye and he relished its tickle on his cheek amidst his beard. He'd earned this sentimental moment, he'd paid his dues. Christ, he *had* earned it. He'd stripped everything out of his life to complete this novel. All distractions removed. Nothing left to chance. Screw the monkeys.

As the printer lazily tongued sheets into its tray, the first page showing the title, *Simian Keys*, he allowed himself a shudder of anticipation – time for the bonfire, the most important of rituals; a part of the media-folklore surrounding Dennis Mann. At the end of every day spent working on a new novel, he would wander out into the grounds of his Catskills writing retreat, gather a bunch of branches and throw them onto a growing pile. Eventually, the pile would become a bonfire. When the novel was complete, Manny (everybody called him Manny) torched the bonfire in celebration, drinking rum from the bottle, spitting it into the flames. It was a pagan thing. The papers loved it. His agent never tired of mentioning it.

It was early evening, but still hot and sticky. Insect orchestras had started warming up. Birds still called back and forth. Manny gathered the final few sticks, choosing interesting or propitious shapes, and then wandered out to the bonfire, holding in his other hand a jerry can whose contents sloshed around as he walked.

He stood before the bonfire, peering at the brute as if it were an opponent in a boxing ring, then tossed the sticks high onto the towering pile. This was no ordinary Mann bonfire; it had been four years in construction. *Four fucking years you have towered over me, hiding me in your shadow*, he thought. *Tonight you burn. Tonight you go back to the ground you sprung from. Ashes to ashes*. He splashed petrol liberally around the base, laughing, arching his back to launch the fuel higher. He lit a match – feeling more tears on his cheeks – said a prayer to the great God of all writers and lit the pyre of his frustrations.

Later, soot-faced and red-eyed, photographed alongside grinning firemen (*Manny, over here... Manny, put on the fire helmet*), while simultaneously being quizzed by journalists who seemed to have covered amazing distances in no time, he admitted he may have used a little too much petrol and far too little caution with the bonfire. He even admitted he could have caused a major forest fire, but the officials were forgiving, understanding, even. This man was a bestseller, a hero. Captain Tucker, head of the firefighting crew, had Manny sign his helmet. He was his number one fan. It made the local news. Later the networks picked it up, and Manny listened to the media drums beating out the message – Dennis Mann was back and he was on fire.

HIS AGENT, Jed Scobey, loved the book. Loved it. Predicted great, *great* things for it. He loved the bonfire incident even more.

"Is this your way of firing me on the sly, Manny? A sort of *Look Jed, I can whip up my own publicity* angle. Just get it out and say it, big guy," he joked, straightening his spotted bow tie. Then, more seriously, because Jed was always serious when he talked about money, "Our people are in communication with their people and in a few days we'll start talking zeroes. Go take a break for a few days."

Manny took Jed's advice, but first he tried to track down Louise, his wife. She'd left Manny two years into the composition of the book and was now tweeting and posting divorce memes. It was time to put her right. She still needed him. She just didn't realise it yet. Posing as a journalist, he tricked Louise's secretary into revealing she was in London, but when she recognised his voice, she refused to divulge any more information. Manny threatened the secretary, her family, and her pets, and she became hysterical, slamming the phone down. She shouldn't have worried; Manny wouldn't have followed through with his threats, he was too much of an animal lover.

HE FLEW TO LONDON ANYWAY. It was a city of many millions, but Louise had particular tastes, and Manny believed in the subtle weave of chance, the power of coincidence; he'd just spent four years writing a book about it – he had to buy into it now. But he didn't find her in any of the galleries he cruised or the theatres he hung around. Never saw the half-smile, half-scowl that was her favoured expression in the crowds he pressed through. As a consolation he picked up a star-struck woman called Anabel – at least half his age, with a Louise Brooks bob – who had been staring at him in a Whitechapel photography gallery. She took him back to her flat and showed him a dozen framed photographs of him she had taken at a signing session eight years ago.

"I was fifteen years old," she said. "My first camera. Not bad, eh?"

Despite the ache in his soul when he looked at the image of his younger, more potent self, he let her photograph him again, bare-chested in her bed as he sucked in his gym-hardened, but irritatingly convex, middle-age spread.

"I can't believe I bumped into you in that gallery," Anabel said later, padding bare-arsed to the kitchen for a glass of wine.

"The power of coincidence," he said, and yawned.

MANNY KNEW there was something wrong when, on his return to New York, he pitched up unannounced at Jed's offices. The receptionist, Mary-Jo, who was usually a model of flirtatious efficiency, let out a birdlike squawk and then flushed red as she paged her boss. Jed called Manny straight in.

"What's the score, Jed? Do we have a problem?"

"The publisher has a problem."

"They don't like the book?"

Jed coughed and rubbed his lips, then investigated an invisible stain on the arm of his jacket.

"Jed! What?"

"No. They love it."

"We asking for too many bucks?"

"Nope."

"What the fuck is it, then? Don't make me jump through hoops, Jed."

Finally, Jed looked up. He spoke, stopped, spread his arms wide and tried again. "They've already bought the book."

"Then what's the problem?"

"They bought it from somebody else."

Manny paused. Rewind. He must have missed something. "What do you mean? *I* am the writer. *You* are my agent. You alone sell my product."

"I mean, they bought it from another author. Some guy called Ethan Banks has written the same book as you. Word for word."

It took a few seconds for the words to register. "Bullshit. You mean he *claims* to have written the same book as me. Christ, I knew this would happen to me one day, some fucker trying for a plagiarism case – well, I'm not even go to mess around with a maggot like that. Not after four fucking years of sweat and pain and then nearly incinerating myself... Christ ... I trust our legal people are talking to his legal people and employing very threatening language as we speak. They are on the case, aren't they, Jed? Jed?"

Manny could not understand Jed's passive expression. The guy was a tiger. He'd expect him to be in full offensive mode. After all this was his livelihood, as well as Manny's, under threat.

"They *were* on the case."

"What do you mean *were*?"

"When did you finish *Simian Keys*?" asked Jed, his voice terse. "Precisely when?"

"You know when. Ten days ago."

"They've had the final corrected proofs of this guy's manuscript for a month. The first draft was delivered seven months ago." Jed stabbed a finger into his desk for effect. Manny heard an expensively manicured nail snap. Jed didn't seem to notice. This was a very bad sign. "The presses and publicity are ready to roll."

"That can't be." Manny felt the words wheeze out of him, as if somebody had punched him on the guts.

"This Banks guy is making noises about suing you if so much as a whisper of this reaches the media."

"Suing *me*." More wheezing words. There was a look in Jed's eyes that made him feel cold and vulnerable. "Don't look at me like that, Jed. I didn't steal the fucking book."

"Of course you didn't, Manny," said Jed, putting on an earnest, supportive face. "This is a bowl of shit, but we don't have to dip our bread in it yet. Go home, don't talk to journalists, don't browse the web and don't read the press. I'll be in touch..."

MANNY WENT HOME, but that was as far as he went in following Jed's advice. The story was already out there, breeding, replicating, mutating, an insidious gossip virus sickening his reputation: *What do you know, the former best-seller whose abilities had waned dramatically over his last three books, finds himself unable to finish a novel for four years and then, out of nowhere – get this – his new novel is mysteriously a word-for-word copy of a new work by an up-and-coming writer. Two books exactly the same. What did they say about monkeys and typewriters and infinite time? And all that business with the forest fire – talk about self-publicity. Some people just can't live away from the glare.*

Manny couldn't sit at home and do nothing. It wasn't his style. He had to fight back, get in some early blows; he had to think like a street fighter. He called a few acquaintances in the press, literary hacks who liked nothing more than carving up a wannabe Young Turk with their sharp, glinting prose, and told them he was about to launch a plagiarism suit against some snot-nosed kid. No, he couldn't go into details about how the kid had got hold of his work... of course this was off the record... what do you mean, are there any fingers pointing at me? I may have been through a bad time, but fuck it, I'm Manny Mann, I don't need to steal, I've still got the juice. And so the beasts were on the scent. One of them emailed him a photograph of Banks. Fresh-faced and virile. Manny deleted it.

"MANNY, I told you to keep schtum – what were you thinking of?" It was Jed, a day later, sounding very pissed off.

Maybe he's found his broken nail, thought Manny, then he said, "I will not lie down and let him do this to me."

At the other end of the line, Jed sighed. "Let me give it to you straight, Manny. At the moment, this kid has all the winning cards. The publisher had his book for months, he's got a score of people who read earlier drafts over the past two years. Two years. He has a one-hundred-percent creative audit trail from the day the light bulb popped on in his curly-headed college-educated brain. You getting this, Manny?"

"I'm getting it," growled Manny.

"As it stands, if I didn't know you, I'd think you must have stolen the book from him. That's how bad it is. I need time to work on this, so help me out by keeping a low profile. Just avoid the bulbs. Can you do that?"

"I can do that."

"Good. Stand by for updates."

———

MANNY TRIED to control his mounting rage and maintain a low profile. He owed Jed that much, and he'd lost any desire to be out and about. His confusion was too great a burden to carry in public. How could this have happened to him? He hadn't stolen Bank's book, he'd never met the man, never wanted to, and stealing somebody else's work... he had been desperate during those four hard years, but not that fucking desperate.

Manny paced around his West Side pad, pounding his heavy bag until sweat flew in every direction, working hard at inverted sit-ups, grunting through scores of push-ups. He inspected his body in profile in a mirror and growled, deciding he'd be better off drinking Scotch.

How to account for what had happened? There was the wildest of probabilities that they could have written the same novel, but the odds were beyond astronomical. Was it something he'd done? The central themes of *Simian Keys* were coincidence and synchronicity; had his writing unleashed some evil statistical juju, a hellish voodoo probability? He chewed over every remote exploration and came solidly to one conclusion: the kid, the fucking kid Banks, was a thief. He was a thief and Manny would tell him so.

Calling in more favours, Manny discovered Banks was giving a series of interviews at a midtown hotel ahead of his book's launch. The usual gig. Journalists sitting around outside a room waiting for their ten minutes of chatter, all the time watched over by a 'helper' representing the publishers. It was time for Manny to speak to his nemesis.

Manny had held lots of interviews in this same hotel; he said hello to the doormen, who nodded nervously in response. The rumour virus had already infected them. He rode the elevator to the designated floor and strode out, sucking in his gut. The man and woman who emerged simultaneously from the lift alongside did not see him. They turned away, towards a room at the opposite end of the corridor where several men and women wearing suits and obsequious smiles stood waiting. The couple turned their faces to reveal their profiles as they kissed – as Ethan Banks kissed Louise Mann. They laughed, smiled and, arm-in-arm, disappeared into the room. They shut the door after them.

Manny literally fell back into the lift.

"Which floor, sir?" said the bellhop.

When Manny didn't answer, he repeated his question.

"The bar," said Manny. "Quickly."

He found the bar and ordered a bourbon. Then another

and another. After that he switched to beer. He had to numb the wild confusion and pain flailing at the edge of his mind, but he needed a little sober section to at least try to wrestle with this latest twist. Had Louise given his book to Banks? She couldn't have; he had written the last third after she stuffed her cases and waggled her ass out the door.

Banks had taken his book, and now he was taking his wife. Who was this guy? He was an absolute bastard.

"You can say that again." It was a female voice at his side. Manny wasn't aware that he'd spoken out loud.

Turning unsteadily, he took one look at the woman sitting next to him – dark bobbed hair and a camera slung around her neck – and slid off his stool.

"What are you doing here? Go back to London," he said from the floor.

"And it's nice to see you too," she said, offering him a hand. "I'm trying to do the same thing as you – trying to see Ethan."

Manny stood up without her help. "Why do you want to see him?"

Anabel gave him a look that implied he was stupid or drunk, or both. "Doh! He's my brother."

"Your brother?"

"Yep, brother, as in egg and sperm from the same parents."

Suddenly Manny felt as though he had drunk three bottles, rather than three shots, of bourbon. The bar whirled around him like a merry-go-round. "He's with my wife."

"I know. Has been for a month."

"Why didn't you tell me in London?"

"Talk about him? I hate the bastard. Anyway, he never talks to anyone about me. In fact, he pretends he's an only child."

Manny grabbed her by the arm and shook her. He didn't know what he was trying to say, or do, but he was seized by an uncontrollable frustration as wild probabilities clustered around him. It was at this moment that the tabloid photographer made his move. Several flashes brightened the interior of the bar, and then he was away with dollar signs spinning in his eye sockets.

THE PAPERS HAD a field day with the breaking story. Celebrated, burnt-out novelist accused by Young Turk (who is bedding the burn-out's recently estranged wife) of plagiarism. The burn-out also seen assaulting the Young Turk's sister in a midtown bar. It made the locals, the nationals and the networks. A crew from the BBC started sniffing about.

When Jed went AWOL and his secretary wasn't able to offer Manny any reasonable explanation, Manny panicked and headed back to his house in the Catskills. Anabel decided she wanted to tag along. For some reason, Manny let her. She'd apologised for startling him in the bar and giving the papers something else to beat him with, and made him laugh when she described the shocked expression on his face. Anyway, the thought of being alone amid all this weirdness was just too stressful.

"I thought you'd burnt that when you finished the book," said Anabel as they approached the house.

The bonfire was back, or more accurately, it had been rebuilt in exactly the same location as before. Someone had raked the ashes of its forebear flat and erected a new pile on top.

"Probably some asshole journalist or photographer," he said.

That night he dreamt of the monkeys again, but this time they were more violent, prying up the roof tiles and screeching for access. He jumped to wakefulness as one of them rang the bell on the porch. His breath laboured with fright, his skin glistened like month-old processed ham. He looked at the woman lying next to him and his mind flailed to recall: who was this? Who had replaced Louise? Then, as his dream head cleared, the warm relief of recognition arrived. He felt the physical warmth of Anabel's body. He stroked her cheek.

The bell on the porch gave a muffled ping, as if some-body had brushed past it and then grabbed it before it could ring fully. Sliding from the bed, straining his ears, Manny crept through the house and peered through a window. There was nobody on the porch, but beyond it he saw the deeper darkness of the bonfire. It was larger than before. *The monkeys*, he thought. *The monkeys are coming for me.*

He went back to bed, curling close to Anabel. When he woke, the whole incident, from the monkeys to the growing bonfire, had acquired the insubstantial texture of dream. While Anabel cooked him breakfast, he wandered out to the porch. The bonfire had definitely been built up. Anabel caught him pouring a Scotch and tutted reprovingly. He poured it back into the bottle.

LATER THAT DAY, they walked through the woods surrounding Manny's house. Anabel happily snapped him, the flora and fauna, and even had Manny take some shots of her as she pouted and posed ridiculously from behind a tree. He found himself laughing again. It was a novelty. He liked it.

Jed still wasn't taking his calls, and a few inquiries to Manny's contacts confirmed what he had suspected: Jed had dropped him. Rumour was that he had hitched his flag to Banks' pole. Some papers were running stories about Manny having a nervous breakdown because he was blocked, others that he was suffering a midlife meltdown. One said that he was screwed up because of adolescent alien abduction. The grounds for a legal challenge did not look firm.

While Anabel griddled chicken on the porch barbeque, the delicious smell wafting by, Manny swung back and forth on the swing bench rereading chapters of *Simian Keys*, remembering the process he had been through to squeeze these words onto the page. They were *his* words. It was *his* story. But what could he do?

Later, rocking side by side with Anabel, sipping whiskey and listening to stories from her life, her expectations of the future, her giddy laugh, watching evening light in her eyes, and feeling something unexplainable stretch within him, Manny had a strange and unsettling thought: *maybe the book's not that important. I'm not going to starve. I could just start again.* A second unexpected thought slid out of hiding and he felt scared – *maybe I can start again with Anabel, in London.* He coughed up whiskey as he forgot to swallow. Anabel slapped him on the back, laughing.

After they'd made love, he held her and watched as she slipped into sleep and thought again: *I do not need this book.*

He slept deeply until the monkeys came back and dragged him to wakefulness, ringing the ship's bell. This time it wasn't echoed by a ringing in the real world, but there was sound, the sound of metal flexing, liquid splashing.

Closing the bedroom door behind him, he crept through the house to the back window. In the moonlight, he saw a monkey. It was large, bent low as it shuffled around the bonfire, pouring liquid from a jerry can. Manny rubbed his eyes and the monkey vanished behind the bonfire. He stepped through the screen door onto the porch. No monkey. A leftover from his dream? No. It emerged from the darkness on the other side of the bonfire, still bent low, pouring, laughing and talking to itself. Manny could smell the petrol.

"Hey," he yelled. "Get the hell out of here."

The monkey turned towards the porch, standing upright and in that same move shedding its simian skin. It was a man. Slowly, he dipped a hand into his pocket and retrieved a small object. A click in the dark and the lighter's flame illuminated the man's face.

"You're a fucking cheat, Manny. It's all lies. Those books were never yours. I was your number one fan. I thought you were the king, man. But all you were doing all those years was butt-fucking me." It was Captain Tucker, head of the local firefighting crew. "I should have let the first fire get you." He raised the lighter higher, replacing his features with shadow. "But there's always a second chance."

When Captain Tucker dropped the lighter, simultaneously leaping backwards, the bonfire erupted into flame. He'd given it a heavy dousing of fuel. But he hadn't stopped there. A trail of fire ran hare-like across the ground, straight towards the house. Manny looked down. He'd thought the boards of the porch were just damp with condensation; now he realised he was paddling in petrol.

"Anabel!" he yelled as he jumped back into the house, feeling the heat of the porch as it was engulfed in flame. Out of the corner of his eyes he could see fire encircling the house. He sprinted down the corridor and flung open the bedroom door. Roiling smoke and fire ripped the breath from his lungs and forced him, arm across his eyes, to back down the corridor.

"Anabel." More of a cough than a shout.

He tried to move towards the bedroom, but the heat was too intense. *This can't happen to me. This can't happen to me.*

He was coughing and whispering. He could see nothing inside but flame and smoke, and already the corridor was too hot to withstand. He backed further away, then, standing to the side of the frame, pushed open his study door. No flames or smoke. He jumped inside. A flickering orange light filled the study windows where the surrounding walls were alight. He burnt his fingers on the window latch but opened the room to the night. Flames tongued their way inside, eager to take the room.

His run up and leap through the window was like a heroic stunt from the movies, except for the fact that he was blinking so much he misjudged his angle, took out a sizable chunk of window frame and wall, and broke his left wrist when he landed. He flapped wildly at the flames in his hair with his right hand.

Staggering away from the burning house, he turned to call out to Anabel. No reply. He was crying again. Tears and flames again. Somewhere in the woods Captain Tucker was crashing through the undergrowth, letting out simian yells of triumph. Manny yelled his frustration into the trees and fell to the ground, cradling his wrist.

The house was already reduced to timbers, collapsing in on itself, on Anabel, spitting burnt flakes and embers into the sky to float between the stars. He'd lost her. He'd barely recognised what she could mean to him and his life, and he'd lost her. Lost everything.

He stood, wincing, and hacked smoke from his lungs. It was a long walk to his nearest neighbour. He had to call the police.

He fell to the ground when he saw Anabel walk towards him out of the wood, pale limbs poking from an oversized white T-shirt, like a cut-price angel. There was a dreamy look on her face. She didn't seem to register either Manny's presence or the burning house.

When he hugged her with his one good arm, covering her with soot, she woke from her dream and gasped.

"What the hell were you doing out there?" shouted Manny, shaking her.

"I must have been sleepwalking. Haven't done it for years. I was dreaming about monkeys. They told me to come and look for them in the woods."

The monkeys. Manny started laughing hysterically.

"What the hell did you do to the house?" said Anabel.

When Manny finally controlled his laughter, he said. "It was the monkeys."

"The monkeys. Do you really have monkeys in the Catskills?" she asked.

Laughter overwhelmed Manny again, closely followed by wheezing coughs. He had to sit on the ground and nurse the jagged pain in his wrist. "Monkeys in the Catskills? Oh, yes. Millions of them."

His laughter filled the spaces between the trees.

CHILDREN OF INK

I am born in pain, blood and ink; beneath the curve of a breast and above the sweet dip of a belly button. A needle, carefully dipped in ink, lowered to my host's flesh. A fearful breath drawn, she's pulling already taut stomach muscles closer to her spine, away from the needle, as if to escape this chosen fate.

You sure about this, Eloise? Half the tattooist's head is shaved and shining, tattooed with words in a seashell spiral: *For the sword outwears its sheath, and the soul wears out the breast.* Long dreads hang down the other side of his face.

For ever and ever, says Eloise.

He lowers the needle to her skin; she emits a girlish squeal of pain, an almost sexual gasp, then a burst of giggles.

Going to be okay with that level of pain? The tattooist dabs blood from the crown of my head.

Tough stuff, me, she says.

Okay, he says. *Here we go, tough stuff.*

It takes hours, but I am born headfirst into this world, on skin raised and raw; the tattoo of a leather jacket-clad man standing atop a name rendered in a gothic font: *Karl*.

A door swings open. Sounds of raised voices and laughter in the reception. Trance- music. Footsteps. A man enters.

Karl, look! says my host, almost squealing with delight as she stretches her torso, stretches *me*, so that Karl can marvel at the tattooist's art.

It's amazing, says Karl. He's bare chested. The right side of his torso is decorated with a fresh tattoo, the surrounding flesh an angry red. I can't get a clear look at it as he bends to inspect me.

Man, that is a-maze-ing, he says, slapping the tattooist on the back. *You made me more handsome than in real life. That's a feat, no doubt about it.*

The tattooist wiggles his fingers. *Magic, man*, he says.

Let me see me, says Eloise.

Karl straightens, turns sideways, raises his left arm above his head and I see his tattoo: an ink woman; tall and slender, sheathed in a clinging slip dress, glancing over her shoulder through a tumble of red hair. A name beneath her feet: *Eloise.*

It's me! shouts my host, sliding from the table, bending for a closer look at the tattoo, her curls tumbling forwards. She sweeps them over one shoulder. *It's really me.*

She stands to kiss Karl. He winds her long red hair in a fist and tugs her head back.

I told you tattoos would be cool, didn't I?

Yes, she says, trying to smile through a grimace.

He leans down to kiss her, her body swinging towards his. I move close to the ink woman. She's on the left side of her host's body, I on the left side of my host's. I can see her out of the corner of my eye. We're cloaked in shadow.

And she winks at me.

The world stops.

She smiles.

Our hosts' bodies move apart.

Did the hosts see? Did they see her wink? Did they see her... move?

No, they're chatting, giggling, pawing each other's bodies, leaning down to inspect us as the tattooist unwraps cling film to bind and preserve us.

I can't believe it. She winked. She smiled.

She moved.

INSTINCT: it's hard-wired into the genetics, into the very essence of every creature. There're some things we don't have *time* to learn in the early hours of life. They just need to be known. A newborn gazelle, gummy and dazed, knows it has to stagger to its feet as quickly as it can to avoid a predator's jaws. The joey has to claw blindly to the pouch. The orangutang has to cling to its mother's body, high in the swinging canopy. Everything has to feed; lips and gums and newly-articulated fingers reach for the nipple and life-giving milk.

It's the same for children of ink. We are born in pain and blood and we know – with an absolute, ink-deep certainty – that visible movement is forbidden. There are Five Laws of Ink:

1. Only move when your host sleeps.

2. Don't let anybody see you move.

3. Always return to the correct place on your host's body.

4. Never leave the body. If a human sees you, disbelief will unmake you.

5. When your host dies, ink dies.

OUR HOSTS RETURN TO A FLAT. I think it belongs to Karl. They pull off their clothes, leaving a textile trail across the living room, giggling momentarily as they slowly remove the protective covers from their tattoos. In the bedroom, my namesake lights a single candle, then falls on my host like an animal on its prey. *No need to rush*, Eloise says, but he pins her arms above her head and bites her. *Please*, she says. *Quiet*, he says.

Later they lie, arms spread as if they are fallen soldiers, sweat drying, chests rising and falling, eyes closed. It's the afternoon. The bedroom curtains are closed, throwing the room into shadow, but it isn't night, it isn't dark. I watch the candle's flame dance and listen to my host breathe. Is she asleep, or just resting? I ache to take my first step, but I do not want to risk breaking any of the Laws. I don't want my life to end before it starts. I ride up and down on my host's body, nervously waiting.

"Hey, lover boy."

Her voice jolts me from my solipsism. I see her, a shadow amongst shadows as she glides across Karl's flesh, crossing from the left side of his torso to the right, close to where I am pressed against Karl's body.

She smiles at me. "What you waiting for?"

I don't know what to do. If I answer, I must move my lips. If I move my lips, I've broken one of the Laws.

"Hello," she says, waving. "You-hoo, is there anybody in there?"

I don't move. I say nothing.

She curls a lip, sweeps her long tumble of red hair over one shoulder. Stares at me. "Goody two shoes, you're no fun."

Then she's moving again, sliding down the side of Karl's body to where his flesh presses against Eloise's. To where it presses against me. I feel her slide against me, body to body, ink to ink, and confusingly, even though we only exist in two dimensions, I can feel her body's curves.

"Let's see if there's any life in you later," she says, planting a kiss on my cheek and sliding back to the far side of her host's torso as he wakes, yawning and reaching down to scratch his crotch.

WHEN ELOISE WAKES, she pulls on a vest top, covering me. I can only see a web of light through the weave of the fabric. She talks and laughs with Karl. They leave the house. Sunlight warms me through cotton. Clinking glasses in a wine bar. The sound of a river. Tooting boats. The glint of a setting sun. More people join them, bodies pressing close as they hug. The vest top peels upwards and faces are pressing in close to see me, back-lit by a roseate setting sun.

Did it hurt?

It's beautiful.

I mean, really, Karl isn't that good looking!

Laughter.

I glimpse ink-Eloise momentarily on Karl's torso, then he tugs down his shirt. I swear she winks at me again.

Light becomes night. They stagger home laughing, shed their clothes again. Karl lights a candle.

Why do you do that? says Eloise.

Candles are magic, he says, pushing her down onto the bed.

I'm too drunk. Too tired, she says.

But Karl's insistent.

That hurts, she says, trying to pull free of his grip.

I love you, he says, covering her mouth when she tries to speak again.

Finally, they lie still. Karl snores. Eloise cries herself to sleep. I wait and wait. I need to be sure they are asleep. I need to make sure they don't see me move. I look out of the corner of my eye, straining to see ink-Eloise on Karl's body, but it's too dark.

"Don't tell me you still haven't moved!" she says, laughing.

I can't see her.

"Behind you, dummy."

I twist my head without thinking. The movement is delicious and sends a narcotic rush of joy through my body.

"See, you can do it."

My jaw literally drops open. She's here, on Eloise's body.

"You left his body."

"Observant, aren't you?"

"The Laws- "

"Laws are for pussies!" she shouts.

"Keep your voice down, you'll wake them."

She laughs. "Wow, you really missed the queue when they were doling out ink-knowledge; only ink can hear ink."

"But- "

"Oh, please, let's not waste time with buts."

She flows upwards across Eloise's breasts, the nipples and aureoles momentarily distorting her features, and comes to rest horizontally across my host's body, her face close to mine. I look up at her. Another rush of pleasure courses through my body.

"Move your body. I dare you," she says, smiling.

I raise an arm to stroke her face, but she pulls away, her

face suddenly convex on the swell of a breast. "Oh no, you haven't earned that yet."

"Okay," I say, ink-deep excitement rattling through me.

I waggle my arms, laughing and closing my eyes as waves of pleasure pulse through me. I wrench my torso sideways and I am unmoored, dancing (badly) across flesh. The sensations are almost too much to take. When I open my eyes I'm gasping, sweating ink. Something gauzy drifts down from Eloise's body and lands on my face. It smells of her – not Eloise, the ink-Eloise. I pull the slip dress from my face and look up. She's naked.

"See, we even control gravity," says ink-Eloise as she floats down towards me, lips parting.

We make love across Eloise's body: across her stomach and between her thighs, crushed in darkness on her back; I chase ink-Eloise the length of my host's legs, across the soles of her feet, I hunt her in the darkness, find her hiding amidst the roots of long red hair. She doesn't return to Karl's body until dawn, when the candle has guttered and died.

SHE VISITS me on Eloise's body every night and we consume each other. I'm in love. There can be no other explanation for the amalgam of excitement and dread that plagues me through the daylight hours; those painfully long hours of ink orthodoxy.

Each night she calls across the shadowy valley between host bodies.

"Come here tonight. You can do it. Leave her body."

Each night I resolve to break the Law. To leap from one body to another. To embrace her on my namesake's flesh. But I don't. I can't.

"Just do it," she teases. "Who'll ever know?"

The answer is: I don't know, or nobody, or does it even matter. But I don't leave Eloise's body because I'm scared. Because I know, instinctively, the Five Laws of Ink; if a human sees me while I'm away from my host's body, their disbelief will unmake me.

Shaking her head, mixing disappointment and seduction in a single glance, she always relents and joins me on Eloise's body. "Oh, Karl."

I try to explain away my fear, but she just shushes me and kisses me and says maybe tomorrow.

"Do you love me?"

I nod and agree and feel sick at the thought of disappointing her again in twenty-four hours.

A TAXI, champagne at the station, giggles and drunken chatter. I can see nothing but hazy light through the weave of a blouse. A train, the darkness of a long tunnel, more wine. Karl stroking Eloise's stomach, my body, his hand moving lower.

Not here, people are watching, says Eloise.

Goody two shoes, says Karl.

We arrive in Brussels. A long weekend. They have been together for two months. There have been arguments and tantrums, one separation and now this trip, a surprise paid for by Karl to help them *get things back on track.* I don't care about any of it except how it affects my access to ink-Eloise.

We arrive at the hotel. They rip off their clothes and embrace beneath the cascade of the rainforest shower. I catch glimpses of ink-Eloise pulling faces at me. Karl drags a giggling, still wet Eloise to the bed, lights a candle.

Gentle, please, she says, but his eyes glaze over and he's pinning her to the bed, slamming against her. He kisses her and rolls away. *Let's go eat,* he says. She sits on the edge of the bed and doesn't speak. He kisses her on the top of the head. *Food?* he says. She nods and slowly bends to pull on her clothes.

That night, as they sleep, I do it.

I slide free of Eloise's body, gliding across the white duvet like a mobile stain, onto the padded headboard and up onto the wall, across wallpaper decorated with dark, branch-like designs intended to make the room feel like an enchanted glade.

I feel high on my love for ink-Eloise, sure that while an emotion this intense runs through my veins nothing... I mean NOTHING... can hurt me – I am ink-Superman.

From my vantage point I watch ink-Eloise cross to Eloise's body, expecting to find me cowering in my usual place beneath her breasts. She stops dead still, stunned by my absence, then, turning her head from side to side, she smiles.

"Yoo hoo!" I wave down at her.

"You finally did it," she calls up. I spread my arms wide and grin.

She joins me on the wall. "Why now?"

"Because of you. You give gave me the confidence."

She leans forward and kisses me. It's a long kiss, deeper than anything we have ever shared before, and this knowledge moves something inside me like a lever beneath a rock.

"Why is he so bloody cruel to her?" she says, nodding at Karl.

I shrug. "What do you mean?"

"Are you blind?"

"What?" I say, genuinely perplexed.

"He hits her. Shouts at her. Forces her to have sex. It isn't a loving relationship."

"Hosts," I say, shrugging, not really understanding her concern. Their behaviour is utterly alien to me. "No point in worrying about puzzles that can't be solved," I say.

"Would you treat me that way?" she says, pouting.

"Have I ever behaved like that?"

"Wrong tense. I'm talking about the future."

"No, I wouldn't, never," I say, dropping to my knees and grabbing her right foot. I pepper it with kisses, biting a toe, and she squeals. Kicks me in the face.

"That hurt," I say, standing, rubbing my cheek.

"Stay still," she says.

"Not playing," I say with a grin.

"Karl!" She hisses the word into my face.

I sense him moving behind me, rocking onto the edge of the bed, scratching his groin, picking a hair from his tongue, yawning, standing, heading for the loo. If he turns around, he'll see us. If he sees us it will unmake us, dot by dot, like each stab of the needle reversed. The birth pain we suffered amplified a thousandfold.

He stops at the doorway, hand on the frame, and looks back to the bed. At Eloise, lying on her front. His eyes are barely open. *Don't look up, don't look up, please don't look up. And don't look at your body.* My unheard words are like a prayer.

He rubs his left eye. Yawns again. Scans the room. I close my eyes. Waiting for the pain to begin. Waiting for it to skewer me and pick me apart.

Urine hammers against porcelain, then water. Karl sighs. Flushes.

"Come on," I say, hurtling down the wall and sliding back beneath Eloise's body. "Hide here, with me."

"What if he sees I'm not there?" ink-Eloise says.

"He won't," I say, but my mind is screaming at me that it's all over. He'll see. His disbelief will unmake ink-Eloise and then, by association, me.

The bed sags beneath his weight as he flops down alongside Eloise.

"Go, now," I say, and she's sliding across the sheets, sobbing with relief.

Neither of us leave our host for the rest of the weekend. The weekend doesn't help their relationship. When we head back to Brighton, ice clings to every sentence they utter.

I SAID NO! Eloise yanks herself free of Karl's grip and rolls off the bed. The room spins around me and steadies as she stands, panting, by the bedroom door. She cradles her left arm, the one he was twisting behind her back.

Karl pushes himself up against the headboard and reaches out a hand, palm flat. As always, there is a candle flickering on his bedside table. He holds his palm an inch above the flickering flame. *Get back here,* he says.

She shakes her head.

Here, now, he says.

No, she says.

This act of defiance has been approaching for a week, rattling through her body like a runaway train. I see ink-Eloise on his body, for once still, obeying the Laws, but I can see the fear in her eyes. She knows what might happen if this goes badly.

Karl sighs, lights a cigarette. Blows smoke at the ceiling. Laughs to himself. *You like it rough.*

No, you. She points at him. *You like it rough.*
Could have fooled me.
Karl, you... I love you, but...
There aren't any buts in love, he says, blowing smoke upwards.
She shows him the bruise spreading across her arm.
He shrugs.
If you hurt me again, I'm leaving you, she said.
He moves like a predator covering the short yards to a kill. Her head smacks against the wall, his fingers around her throat, palm hot from the candle, breath hot on her cheek, body close to hers.
"We have to go, now," says ink-Eloise – our hosts' bodies press too tightly together for me to see her, but I can hear her panicked voice. "We have to go before something bad happens, something terrible."
I decide; she's right. I want to be with her all the time and rules are for pussies. I flex my arms, feeling the usual adrenaline thrill, and get ready to leap onto Karl's body.
Bitch! Karl is stumbling backwards, bending over and folding ink-Eloise in half, clutching his groin, a grimace crumpling his face.
It's over! Eloise is yelling, gathering her clothes, scrambling from the bedroom.
I see ink-Eloise's mouth moving. I try to read her lips. I can't.
The bedroom door slams behind Eloise and she's bounding downstairs, glancing over her shoulder, twisting her ankle, cursing, hobbling out onto a rain-wet pavement. Dawn light. Bloody clouds. Fumbling car keys into the door, the ignition. The engine coughing to life.
We leave. It starts to rain.

ELOISE DOESN'T RETURN his call, nor does she return to his flat. Two days pass. She cries and talks to friends on the phone. Her best friend, Orla, comes to stay.

I've brought aromatherapy candles, to help you relax, says Orla, holding up two brightly-coloured wax cylinders.

No candles! snaps Eloise, then plunges her face into her hands, shoulders rising and falling with sobs.

They drink wine and talk and cry some more.

I'm paralysed by fear, by an ache I cannot name or tame.

I need to see her again.

Eloise! A voice shouting up from the street.

Orla peeks out the window. *It's him.*

Ignore him, says Eloise.

He continues to call for her, the pitch of his voice shifting towards something dark and violent. I have a wild urge to slip from Eloise's body and jump up onto the windowsill. To peer down and see her, even though, rationally, I know Karl won't be standing in the street bare-chested.

He's thumping the front door, demanding an audience with Eloise. Orla calls the police. Screams down at him from the first floor. A window breaks. The police arrive. There's shouting and scuffling. Car doors slam. The police drive away. Eloise is crying again.

FOR TWO DAYS I am immobile with indecision. I remain perfectly still, true to my ink, not so much as curling a finger. Even when Eloise sleeps, her head resting on a tear-damp pillow, I am only a pattern decorating her flesh.

What is the best course of action: should I wait for the chance of reconciliation between the warring lovers? Or should I slip away from Eloise in the night and strike out across the city to be with ink-Eloise? I know the location of Karl's flat. They always met there. Ink-Eloise doesn't know where Eloise lives. The two options tip up and down in my mind, inconstant weights on the scales of action.

I question myself: my courage, my fortitude, my love for ink-Eloise. Is this really indecision? Or is this fear?

Karl leaves messages on the house phone. The police let him out without charges after a night in a cell. He wants to see her again. He *needs* to see her again. He forgives her.

Forgive me! Eloise screams, throwing the phone against the wall so hard it splinters into black plastic shards and a shower of electric components. *Fuck you!* She stamps on the remains of the phone and collapses onto the sofa, sobbing. In that moment of rage and denial, I hear need. The first crack in her resolve. They will get back together. I know they will, and I know how to expedite the reunion.

That night I leave her body. Sliding across the duvet, I reach her mobile phone. I have little mass, but it is enough to operate the virtual keys on a smartphone.

We are bound by our tattoos, I type. *I am on you; you are on me. We are the same.*

Smiling, I return to her body.

HE DOESN'T CALL.

It takes two more days for *her* to call *him*.

Ear to her phone, a ringtone. A cigarette flutters between her fingers. She raises it to her lips. Smoke hisses between her teeth.

What? I can just hear his tinny voice escaping the phone.

Hi babe.

What do you want?

I'm sorry, okay, she says.

I'm not.

Not what?

I'm not sorry.

What do you mean?

It's all down to your text.

Eloise pauses, confused. *What text?*

Yeah, right.

I don't know what you're talking about.

It showed me the way forward.

Babe, I don't understand.

Don't call me babe.

But...

We weren't right for each other. I've moved on. I've got somebody else now.

There's silence for long seconds. When she speaks, her voice sounds like dead branches cracking. *It's only been a week.*

Time waits for no man. I'm going now. Don't call back.

The ringtone.

No, no, no. She's squeezing the phone until the plastic creaks.

She calls back. They argue and he cuts her off.

She calls back again, and he cuts her off before a word can escape her lips.

She dials again.

Wait, don't hang up, she says.

Then he speaks. I can't hear everything he says – his

voice is low and menacing – but I make out the words *text* and *tattoo*.

He hangs up. She doesn't call back. Lying in bed, sobbing, she stares at her phone, as if she expects a message to light its screen at any second. It doesn't.

What did he say to her?

She dials a friend's number but hangs up before speaking. Plays loud – no, *very* loud – music. It throbs through the house like a giant's heartbeat. She drinks red wine. Way too much wine. She calls Karl's number and leaves a message on his answerphone. My ink goes cold.

She can't be serious.

She's drinking more wine, pulling her dress over her head, hair tangled in the zip, ripping out a chunk. She's standing in front of the bathroom mirror wearing panties and bra. Her faces screws up. She growls as she scrapes a nail across my - his -face. It's agony, but I don't move. More tears. She's rattling pills from a bottle. Swallowing them one by one.

I can't let her do this. The text – I sent the text.

Only ink can hear ink.

I do the only thing I can do: I move. I move and I let her see me move. I jump up and down, hands raised and waving, mouthing the words: *Don't do it.*

She drops the bottle of pills and it shatters. White oblongs skitter in every direction. She leans against the opposite wall and, like a terrible actress in a horror film, rubs her eyes, removes her hands, opens her eyes, refocuses and screams.

I try to tell her it was my fault; I sent the text. She wraps a towel around her body to cover me. I slide upwards, emerging on her shoulder, and she whimpers in horror, dropping to the floor to scoop up handfuls of pills.

Mad, she says to herself. *I've gone mad. No more no morenomore.*

She sobs and swallows pills and wine and wine and pills and lies down on her bed, humming along to the deafening music. She shuts her eyes tight. At first her breath comes hard and fast – she's almost panting – but then it slows, and her body becomes still.

I did this. Shit, shit, shit! I did this.

She's dying.

I did this.

Law 5: When your host dies, you die.

I slide onto her face and yell into her ear, pleading with her to wake, to call an ambulance, but there's no point; only ink can hear ink.

I have no choice. I have to leave her body for good – I have to *renounce* her. Somehow, I know this is the right word; if a tattoo leaves its host's body permanently, it *renounces* the host – more hard-wired survival instinct. If she isn't my host, I won't die. And I'm not ready to die. Not while ink-Eloise is out there.

A breath rattles from Eloise's mouth and I do it – I jump (as close as you can come to jumping in two dimensions), leaving a trail of ink tears, each a single stab of the needle, across her chest.

I'm on the quilt, the bed frame, the carpet, the electric thrill of movement coursing through me, making me sick with guilt and shame as my former host lies dying behind me and it's all my fault. I feel like a junkie sneaking away after stealing from a dying pensioner.

But what else can I do?

I FLEE THE FLAT. Eloise's road is lit by streetlamps and a slender moon. There are plenty of shadows . I slide quickly between them, waiting and watching whenever a host passes. I follow my mental map towards Karl's flat, but my progress is slow. There are so many hosts. I come to a street lined with bars and restaurants spilling music and light. Hosts cluster outside, talking animatedly, the blue tips of e-cigarettes like fairy lights. There's too much light. I divert into side streets. I lose my way, double back, start again. My journey to ink-Eloise becomes an epic quest.

I tire; I didn't know I *could* tire. I find a graffiti-deco-rated alleyway in which to rest The streetlights only reach the entrance, leaving most of it in deep shadow. I close my eyes. Ten minutes; I'll rest for ten minutes.

"Where're you yomping to, soldier?"

I look up. A graffiti cat skillfully crafted from half a dozen sprayed black lines stares down at me. Manga-sized silver irises engulf pinprick pupils.

I slide away from the wall.

The cat laughs. "Uh oh. A fresh *renouncer* scared of shadows."

"You can talk?" I say, confused.

"So can you." The cat tips its head to one side.

"But... you're just graffiti."

"Just? *Just*! Man, I hate tattoos, you're all so bloody self-centered. Me, me, me, me." The cat scowls as he stretches towards me, claws extending. "You get a couple of TV shows dedicated to you and you're convinced you're the only art with any life."

"You can move," I say, knowing how dumb I sound, but fear and exhaustion trips my tongue.

The cat hisses. "Ink, paint, pencil and sculpture. We can

all move, idiot. Long as we obey the Laws. We're all the same. Except for one thing. Know what that is?"

I shake my head.

"Tattoos taste the best."

The cat moves quick as spray from a nozzle. His body narrows as it arrows towards me, as if air pressure is pushing its lined contours together. I scream as he bites into my right arm. Teeth meet and I fall back, hand clasped over a stump ending where my bicep recently bulged. The cat drags my limb back to the wall, leaving a trail of inky blood, and gnaws on it, smiling around the morsel.

I scream at him, an incoherent and impotent sound.

"I'd run if I were you. I'm coming for more when I finish this." Ink bones crunch as the cat gobbles the arm up to the wrist. "This is just the start."

I slide across the alley floor, speeding out into the street beyond, inky blood leaking around my fingers.

"I like the thrill of the chase!" shouts the cat.

I flee blindly, losing all sense of direction. The city is a maze. I'm fuelled by fear. Lights spin around me. Striding hosts. The noise of cars and buses. Dawn rising. Shadows softening. There's no sign of the cat pursuing me.

My arm has stopped bleeding, but it's so painful I can barely form a thought. I know I can't risk being out in the day. I slide beneath the door of a derelict shop, amidst piles of rotting mail, dust, rat droppings and random detritus. I crawl into the corner of the room, hold my stump and cry. How could this have happened to me? I'm utterly exhausted. I need to rest. I close my eyes. Sleep takes me.

My eyes snap open. I hear something. Inside the shop. The light filtering through the shuttered windows is tinged red: sunset; I've slept all day.

I hear the sound again. I spin, searching for motion.

"The Big Cat's looking for you." The voice is jagged, rusty. "He's offering a reward."

"Dead or alive." Another voice. Laughter like blown plaster rattling between old walls.

"Who's there?" I say, moving towards the door.

A broad strip of moldy wallpaper sloughs from the wall and uncurls towards me. A flickering shadow rides its crest like a surfer. There are things sliding along the far wall, stuttering motion between bars of shadow. They're faded and menacing, weather-worn graffiti remnants; the graffiti walking dead.

I'm out of the shop and blinking against a ruby sunset before they can get close to me with their grasping hands, but I don't stop. I flee blindly, taking corners at random. Glancing over my shoulder. No sign of pursuit. I embrace the city maze.

I arrive at a major road. When I see the road sign above me I almost cry out with joy. I know this road. I know it leads to the western suburbs: it leads to Karl's apartment.

IT'S late evening by the time I arrive at the apartment. From street level I can see a light on in his bedroom, in *her* bedroom.

"I'm coming," I say out loud, then glance over my shoulder as prickling intuition signals a proximate threat. I scan the shadows expecting to see Big Cat's grin, or the flicker of graffiti zombies, but there is nothing visible.

I slide beneath the building's entrance door and ride carpeted stairs to the top floor, into the apartment, into the bedroom, up the wall to gain a vantage point over the bed. The candle on the bedside table throws dancing light onto the two entwined bodies. Karl atop a short, heavy-limbed woman, eyes closed, Louise Brooks bob clinging to her sweaty brow. And amidst the flickering shadows I can see two ink figures grappling with each other as they screw on Karl's back. One is another me, another ink-Karl, similar but not the same; a clone with a subtly tweaked DNA – ink-Karl 2. I recognise the female, her voluptuous curves, the long red hair, but I do not recognise the manic movements, the way she claws at ink-Karl, rakes him with her nails. Ink-Karl 2 tries to pull away from her lacerating nails and they tumble across Karl's back. I see her face. I see what he has done to her. Gone are the bowed lips and sparkling eyes. In their place are a demon's features: scarred cheeks, green flesh, horns curling from her forehead. Red eyes filled with madness. He has destroyed both Eloises.

My vision darkens. My missing arm throbs, desperate for action. Desperate to close fingers around Karl's throat and squeeze until he stops breathing. I cannot do this, but I can do something worse.

KARL WAKES and rolls sideways into a sitting position on the side of the bed. He scratches his chest and groin, then glances over his shoulder at the woman lying on her front beside him. He slaps her already bruised arse. She groans.

Leave me alone.

He laughs and staggers to the bathroom, rubbing his eyes. Takes a piss. Turns to the sink and drinks from the tap. Looks at himself in the mirror. His mouth moves soundlessly. He splashes water on his face and blinks. Scratches the two tattoos on his chest.

No, no, no.

He's back in the bedroom, flipping the protesting woman onto her back, her flesh wobbling then settling.

Get off me. I'm too sore, she says.

He paws the flesh beneath her breasts, where the tattoo of ink-Karl 2 has been stabbed into her flesh. The flesh is pristine. Clean of ink.

The woman sees his chest and looks down at her own body, incomprehension clouding her eyes.

What? is the only word she can summon.

How did you do this? Karl yells.

I didn't do it, you dickhead, she yells back.

His arm is lithe as a whip. Her head jerks to the side and she's cursing him at the top of her voice.

Karl doesn't care. He's back in the bathroom. Scratching at the tattoo corpses on his chest. Naked Ink-Karl 2 has been messily decapitated. Pools of blood ink pool around his ragged neck. Broken and twisted limbs. Ink-Eloise, with her devil-mutilated face, lies peaceful, fully clothed, arms folded across her chest like a body at a wake.

Beneath their bodies is a message written in blood ink.

You are a murderer!

Karl screams like a child lost in a nightmare.

———

I LEAVE THE FLAT. Dawn is grey and flat, the sun hidden behind tower blocks. People are waking. Car doors slam and engines gun to life. Radios burble behind closed windows. It's no time for a tattoo to be about, but what do I care? I've crossed a line. I've changed.

I sense Big Cat behind me before he speaks.

"Look at the ink stains on you. Looks like you've been up to serious no good," he says, stalking towards me, mouth opening, sharp teeth catching the first rays of sunlight. Graffiti zombies flicker in the shadows beneath a parked van.

"Wait," I say.

"Why should I?" says Big Cat.

"Because if you don't, I'll rip your head off."

Big Cat laughs. "You know, I think I could find some work for a one-armed enforcer with a freshly-minted badass attitude. Interested?"

"Depends on the pay," I say.

"Let's talk," says Big Cat, turning with a flick of its tail. "I've always had a soft spot for renouncers."

»

WEARING SKIN

No!

Oh, please God, no. What have I done? Can't be. Can't be. Can she?

(His vision clears. Red mist hazing to reveal the red floor. The red body.)

Why? Oh God oh God oh God. This isn't me. Not like this. I couldn't't have. I couldn't't... I couldn't't... Tell me I couldn't't. Not in me. No violence.

A lie.

(He's kneeling down by the body, wet road dampening his knees. Thickening blood gluing her long hair into slick dreadlocks. Violence has driven bone inwards – splintering it, cutting into her brain – but some shards protrude outwards and, in the moonlight, they are tooth-white. A mouth on the back of her head. Is this how the dead scream?)

Why didn't you tell me? At the beginning. You had the time, so much bloody time. There was no need to lie. If I'd known from the beginning, I could have tried to understand. Slowly. We had time. You of all people should have appreciated that.

Time.

(He's stroking her head. Blood on his fingers. He's crying, looking up at the night sky, the moon, cubist-distorted through his tears. He sobs.)

I made it impossible, didn't I? Me. I killed you the first moment I met you. You would never be able to tell me.

Me.

I SCURRIED, switching from pavement to tarmac to avoid loud groups of drinking, giggling men. Testosterone (I suppose) hung like a cloud over the roadside tables. It was early evening, but still hot. The sun flared off windows into my eyes and I had to squint and use my hand as a visor. Tanned bodies in tight shirts everywhere. How the fuck did they all find the time to work out? I'd like a body like that, but there weren't enough hours in the day. Maybe they were born with a workout maximization gene.

I craned my neck above the crowd to see if she was waiting, ready to pounce on me. I knew this was one of Annie's mind games; I'd heard the amusement in her voice when we'd arranged where to meet over the phone. She loved games, testing me, and I loved showing her that her tests would never disprove my certainties. No way. She could have picked anywhere in Soho, or in London, but she chose here, just so she could accuse me of the modern heresy – the B word. But I wasn't a bigot. I just disliked the excess abandon of gay culture, especially on streets like this. It was so loud and brash; the trashy and cheap raised up as icons. It was an aesthetic thing. Nothing to do with sex, or fear of their sort of sex. But to raise any objection to the way any minority lived these days was tantamount to... I don't know. Setting fire to an Andrex puppy.

I heard a hand slap flesh and a bare-chested man, shirt flapping around the torso of a Greek sculpture, jumped across my path and into the road. He laughed, mugged an angry expression and pointed at the red welt rising above his pierced left nipple. Instead of walking through the confrontation I stepped out into the street and around the man. It was the polite thing to do, I thought. For my troubles I received a derisive whistle, a catcall and a gale of laughter. I looked at my watch. I was late. I sped up.

ANNIE WAS STANDING outside the bar, leaning against a wall, bottled beer in one hand, looking down the street away from me. She was wearing a short, strappy dress and Converse. She stood on tiptoes to scan for me, stretching those lovely legs to even greater length, and I felt the thump of sexual need in my solar plexus – I needed her flesh like I needed to breathe. I remember the first time I met her in the crush of a Saturday-night bar, her body as sinuous as smoke as she wound through the crowd, far too elusive for all the men who tried to grasp her. Except me. That night I breathed her deep into my lungs. Cool, heady smoke.

I don't know what she hoped to see this evening. Me, hugging the broken white line at the centre of the road, or struggling through the crowd in a contamination suit. For sure, she expected me to fail her test. I knew her; I knew her so well it hurt or, often, made me want to hurt her. Just to prove the point, I watched her tip her head back to drink and then... *here it comes... da-da!* – she tucked wayward strands of hair behind both ears, two combs with her fingers on both sides. Every time. Gotcha! I sneaked up and pinched a wonderfully tight buttock.

As usual, our time together became a competition. She had to prove she was smarter, more moral, healthier, a heap more well-adjusted than me. I don't know why she persisted in going out with me if I was so subhuman. I don't know why I persisted with her arrogance, and I'd lost count of the times I had resolved to move on, saving myself the grief of jumping through her hoops. I shouldn't have worried. I didn't know it just yet, but this would be the terminal exchange of our relationship.

The competition continued, then things got worse. She slipped into philosopher mode. Four drinks and she was a right Kant. I said that to her once, and we didn't speak for a week.

"Imagine a sister and brother," she said.

"A brother and sister for myself?"

"No. Any sister and brother. Two people. A brother and sister who are very close." She waved a hand drunkenly. "Any two people."

"Is this a ménage à trois?"

"Of a kind. Here's the thing. Love and hate. Absolute love and hate. You and the sister love each other absolutely. You cannot live without each other. *But* you and the brother hate each other absolutely. The town ain't big enough for both of you. One of you will have to die."

"This sounds plausible."

"Shut up. It's theoretical. So, in a situation like this, what wins out?"

"Go with the girl. Fuck the brother."

"You can't. Your hate for the brother means you can't

just ignore him. It'd eat you up from the inside. A cancer of hate."

"Well then, I don't know..." I was already bored with the game. "Kill the brother and go with the girl."

"You can't – she loves her brother, too. Kill the brother, lose the sister."

"I guess I'd just top myself and save the hassle."

Annie stamped a foot petulantly. "You're so infantile. Think it through. Argue with me."

"Annie, it's all bollocks."

That was it. The end of Annie. Other words were spoken, but we were drunk and our words were just filling spaces. We decided to leave.

We crossed the road, making our way towards the tube, still bickering drunkenly, and it was only at the last moment we saw the two people sprinting towards us. Ten metres away. A man chasing a woman. He was tall, bald, with an angular face red from exertion. She was short and slender, with muscular legs. Unusual red patterns decorated her white T-shirt. Intense concentration pinched her features towards the centre of her face. Bizarrely, she reminded me of an athlete, a long jumper or pole vaulter on the run up. Five metres. I grabbed Annie's arm to pull her out of the way, but typically, fatally, she pulled against me.

They collided with us. The woman ran straight into Annie, forcing her down and, as she still held tight to my hand, pulling me after her. The man clattered against my arse and spun up and over. I heard him slap onto the pavement. Tears filled my eyes as my nose hit concrete. Fluid running into my hand. I sat back on the pavement and sneezed, massively. Annie, features screwed tight, legs kicking, was frantically trying to pull herself free from the woman lying prostrate across her. Annie's dress now had red patterns on it. How so? I rubbed the tears from my eyes. Looked at her dress and my hands. It was blood. Blood leaking from the woman's stomach. And she wasn't moving, except for the jolts as Annie kicked.

She's dead. Ohmygod, she's dead.

The man was climbing unsteadily to his feet, swaying as he turned to face us. He glanced at me and then his head lolled towards Annie. He smiled. I saw the knife in his hand. A bead of blood hanging from its tip.

Then, shouts from across the road. Unforeseen saviours. Two coppers. As adrenaline pumped within me, I saw them with hyper-clarity: white short-sleeved shirts with chromatographic sweat rings at the armpits, stab vests, belts carrying truncheons and tools, topped by blue helmets with their blessed silver nipple. A radio squawked. Bloody saviours.

The angular-faced man hissed at us, turned and legged it.

I threw one of my ripest insults after him and started shaking.

Annie collapsed.

DEATH CHANGES YOU; it helps you to slough off layers of triviality and pretentiousness; it humbles you and makes you more human – at least, that's what I thought accounted for Annie's behaviour when I took her back to my flat. Paramedics had checked us for injuries – Annie coming around quickly, blinking, shaking – and then the police had driven us to a station to give statements. I asked after the woman in the white t-shirt; the paramedics had been applying cardiac massage as we'd driven away. A policeman told me she'd died at the scene, blood loss from a knife wound to her stomach. The angular-faced man had disappeared.

"Take me home," Annie had said.

"Back to your flat?" I'd asked.

She'd looked confused. "No. Take me home with you. Please. I'm scared."

Then she held me tight. Squeezed me. And when I hugged her back, she'd sighed and relaxed a little, as if I'd passed on some of my strength to her. I'd never had that feeling with her before. She'd never been so silent. I took her home. I took *her* home, not Annie, but I didn't realize it yet.

She woke screaming around three o'clock in the morning. I lurched into wakefulness and held her again, trying to calm her.

"He's here," she whispered. She was looking into the dark corners of my bedroom. Head snapping left and right.

"There's nobody here." I turned on a bedside light. "Look, nobody here; it was just a nightmare."

Her eyes were wide open, still focusing on the end of a dream. Slowly, she focused on me, there and then. Even then there was something absent and foreign to her. The way she held herself just wasn't right. Maybe she was in shock. I considered driving her to the local A&E but before I could speak, she smiled briefly, sighed and lay back down, pulling me close to her. I turned off the light.

"Hold me," she said.

I held her tight to comfort her, but that indefinable change unsettled me. To my incident-drunk mind it was like sleeping with a stranger, frighteningly arousing. The erotic frisson of the unknown. I tried to stop myself, but it was no use. My cock pushed against her leg. At first, I thought I'd escaped, that she'd fallen asleep, but her hand slid between us and held me, squeezed tightly once and then released me.

"Not now," she said.

"I'm sorry. I didn't mean to..." I stammered into silence. Had I ever apologised to Annie before?

VERY EARLY THE FOLLOWING MORNING, I awoke alone in bed. Had she left me, my strange new Annie? I panicked and shambled into the living room, then on into the kitchen. She was sitting there in the pale morning light, her back to me, watching the steam rising from a mug of coffee. She was wearing one of my T-shirts, nothing else. Her long hair fell alongside her face and she raised her hands to tuck it behind her ears, two quick combs with her fingers on both sides. I felt a stab of sorrow at this familiar tic, a pinprick to deflate the previous night's sense of mystery and change. The old Annie was back.

"Annie?"

She didn't reply, just let the steam bathe her face. Then I noticed that her hands were gripping the edge of the table, knuckles blanched by pressure, shoulders bunched. I repeated her name and still she didn't respond.

When I placed a hand on her shoulder, any trace of the old Annie evaporated. The chair legs screamed against the floor as she twisted and pulled away from my touch, eyes wild, seeming to focus simultaneously near and far. She huddled against the wall, teeth chattering, shivering.

"Hey, it's okay," I said, squatting down alongside her and slowly reaching out my hands, showing them to her, trying not to startle her. "It's me. It's okay."

I slid my arms around her, and although she

consented to allow her body to fall towards mine, it was still hard and distant. I hummed comforting words as I rubbed her back and moved my hands higher, stroking her hair.

"It's all right. It's all over now. That was last night. He's gone. Nothing to do with us."

I slid my fingers into her hair and massaged her scalp. And that is when I heard it for the first time. The moment it truly began. I heard the terrible sound as if it were in my head. It vibrated out of her, shuddering through my finger bones, arms, jaw and skull. A deep bass, wavering note, the lowest note from a church organ with pipes playing a hymn of terror. My vision blanked out everything except Annie's hair. I was falling into it, into her head, into the sound and utterly primal fears.

Panic.

Flee.

Cry.

Hide.

Quiver and whimper.

Come to me...... let it end......

I would have run blindly, screaming from the terror, if I hadn't been so afraid of my movements alerting it to my presence. Of letting its eyes fall upon me. The note swallowed time. Gradually, it diminished. Moving away, maybe. Fading until it was only the faintest of background noise and then nothing. Early morning birds, a car's engine coughing into life, a neighbour's radio.

Gasping, I fell away from Annie as she sobbed and rocked herself.

"So close again," she whispered and looked at me with eyes full of desperate pleading. "So close."

I quieted my panting fear. "It's over now," I said,

although I did not understand what there was to have ended.

She smiled, briefly. "Take me back to bed and hold me, please."

And so I did. She pulled herself into a foetal position and I held her as best as I could.

Her eyes were closed when she said: "I'm not Annie anymore. I took her body."

"I know," I said and watched her release a quivering sigh.

"Sleep," she said.

I DREAMED THEIR STORY. I'm sure that it wasn't a dream stumbled upon randomly. More likely she'd hung these pictures in the gallery where my sleeping mind roamed. It was a story that could only be explained with dream images, only accepted when I was in that most receptive of states.

The first of them came into being over two thousand years ago, or so their legends said, when a small tribe walked through the shadow of a god, cleaving their souls from their bodies. Now they were free to abandon their shells when the need arose, to inhabit another body, working free the owner-soul like a mollusc from its shell, casting it aside, replacing it. Wearing skin. As long as they fled a body before it expired, their souls were immortal. To stay inside a dying body pulled them into oblivion.

Back then, the world lay before these newborn immortals. An orchard of lives to satisfy their hunger for all the sweet things in creation. But they realised the blessing that had fallen upon them came with a responsibility, and so they created laws to guide and govern their actions. The most important of the laws governed the procurement of bodies, the taking of fresh skin. On this they were all agreed – they would only take the bodies of those who were sad. People sick of life, afraid to live, unable to cope with the rush of the world. They would repeat the code to each other as a blessing. *We only take the sad.*

On rare occasions, these souls encountered others capable of the same mobility. This was time for a celebration. They welcomed these newcomers into the tribe, educated them to their gift and taught them their laws.

Slowly, the tribe grew, splitting and seeding the world. They would always be the smallest of minorities, the most secret of societies, but their influence would be felt in the roots of myth and legend and fairy tale. People would be burnt at the stake for possession, as a newcomer to the tribe struggled to evict a soul from its host; some would see imprints of evicted souls staining reality as ghosts; tribe members who had lived centuries and were slowly turning mad, seeking something new in the world, would prowl the night drinking blood; others inhabited the bodies of wolves, tigers or bats to terrorize non-immortals. They passed into myth, then literature, then cinema, leaving story-struck non-immortals to imitate them. A great fiction celebrating, but misinterpreting, the greatest of secrets.

The rarest of events was a soul that rebelled at the wonderful possibility lying before it. For the sake of the tribe's continued secrecy, they destroyed such souls. No recalcitrant had ever escaped this fate, except for one: Ezekiel Jeremiah. He could have been one of their greatest. The tribe saw the gift in him. He had a powerful soul. But what the tribe did, and what he became, soon left him appalled. He preached against their practices. Railed at them to renounce their immortality.

The tribe knew they had to act, but they had underestimated his strength and conviction. They made plans to confront him, but Jeremiah attacked first. He struck down three of the strongest immortals, gutting them before they had time to flee their dying bodies, condemning them to a permanent end. He vanished into another body before the others, terrified by the enormity of what they had witnessed, could organise a counterattack. Ever since that day, Jeremiah had haunted their world, growing stronger and more resolute, hunting down the members of the tribe one by one, *relieving the world of the burden of immortals*. It was Jeremiah's soul that sang the terrible hymn of oblivion in their thoughts as he hunted them down. As he closed in for the kill.

WHEN I WOKE, she was looking at me, hugging her knees, waiting for me to speak. There was a different fear in her eyes. I did not know what to say.

"Do you hate me for what I've done to Annie? For what I am?" she asked.

I thought I knew the answer to this question: "No."

Later, we walked for hours in the park. Her hand found mine and she told me stories of her tribe, the women she had been and the people she had known, the events she had witnessed. My doubts unraveled amidst her wondrous stories.

"Do you have Annie's memories?" I asked.

She shook her head. "No. I tasted some of them when I entered her, but they are bound up with the soul. There's nothing left of her but this." She ran her hands over her body. "But I know enough of her to say she was an unhappy person. We only take the sad."

Nor had I been a happy person. But unexpectedly, I had a hope that this might change. "What shall I call you? I mean, what were you called... originally."

"The original is long gone. Call me Annie."

By the end of the walk, my body was trembling with hunger; I had not eaten since the previous lunchtime, but the stress and strangeness of events had wiped out the need until now. Annie said she was hungry too. We found an Indian restaurant and gorged ourselves on rich food and cold beer. And still we talked. It was as heady as a first date laced with the sense that it would end amidst sweat-soaked, tangled sheets.

As we prepared to leave the restaurant, she grabbed my hand and looked hard into my eyes. I still could not quite believe all these fresh gestures from this familiar body.

"Do you really accept me for the truth of what I am?" she said.

"Yes," I said, not entirely truthfully, for how could I hope to understand such a mystery so quickly?

Like a dream, naked in the candlelight, she climbed across the bed and straddled me. The combination of the familiar and the unknown made me lose my mind. When we stopped to rest, I had no words. I squeezed her face, as if my fingers might pull clay from her frame. When nothing happened – how could this be? – I squeezed harder. She prized my fingers away and comforted me, then made love with the ferocity of somebody wishing to test the limits of a physique. Later she bent forward, tilting her hips, looking over her shoulder as she presented her spread cheeks. I pushed into the orifice she was offering, relishing its tight grip. My release was sweet and savage.

We didn't leave the flat for the next two days. I called work and claimed to be sick, reeling from the shock of the murder I had witnessed. I neglected to mention that I was blissfully trapped in tangled sheets with a murderer.

We ate, made love, and slept. Between each bout of pleasure, she told me more tales of the tribe. With all the knowledge they possessed, she could reach beyond the unsteady extrapolations of historians to retrieve first-hand or word-of-mouth accounts of the truth. The language she used danced, its vocabulary and intonation and passion far removed from the hectoring delivery of the original Annie. Her voice was music. She told me one of the tribe had been the driver who had smuggled Elvis to a life incommunicado. Another gone mad had been the Ripper, pulling apart bodies, looking for imperfect souls to chew upon. Gandhi and William the Conqueror shared the same soul and David Soul was immortal – I think the last one was a joke.

I loved every story about the tribe, and I thought I loved the tribe, until Raul arrived in London and broke the selfish spell.

"I can hear him," squealed Annie with delight. "It's Raul. I'm sure it's Raul. So faint, but he's here. He's looking for me. I told him I would stay in London. I told him."

Immediately, Annie wanted to venture out into central London – *he'll wait for me in the crowds*, she said. *That way it's more difficult for Jeremiah to hear us.* I tried to persuade her to stay with me in the house, arguing it was still too dangerous. Jeremiah could be closer than she thought. She wasn't ready yet. Even she admitted that she didn't fully understand Annie's body. But I could not dissuade her. Raul was one of her oldest friends.

WE WANDERED the West End for three hours as Annie zeroed in on the sound of Raul's soul. Despite her joy at the prospect of seeing an old friend, I could see the attentive fear on her face; we were close to where she had last, and almost fatally, encountered Jeremiah. Annie stopped at the base of Nelson's Column, cocking her head, listening. I asked her what she could hear. She placed my fingers on her head and again her thought vibrations worked their way into me. But this time, rather than the overpowering terror of Jeremiah, I could hear a babble of millions of distinct notes, the sound of the city's body-locked souls. Amidst all this was one note that sounded clear and consistent above the others.

"That's Raul," she said, then hesitated. "And I can hear another."

"Jeremiah?" I asked.

"Oh no."

"Who, then?"

"Another one of the tribe." Annie looked troubled.

We found him amidst the camera-slung scrum of tourists at Cambridge Circus, head bent back to take in the beautiful facade of the Cambridge Theatre. He was taller, younger and more powerfully built than I was – or, I should say, his borrowed body was. He could have been as old as Herod.

"I like the new chassis," he said, sweeping Annie into his arms and squeezing her arse. "Not to your normal taste..."

"Annie," she said, interrupting him. "I'm called Annie."

"You can call yourself whatever you desire, but you don't mind if I just stick with Raul, do you?"

"You'll always be one hundred percent Raul whatever skin you wear."

"Skin *schmin*" he said, holding Annie in his arms then, laughing, twirling her on the spot so that tourists had to jump out of the way of her sweeping legs. Annie giggled like a schoolgirl. He put her down and leered at her with an expression that would have better suited a dirty old man. "Who's the lifer?" he said, finally acknowledging my presence.

"Matt," I said before Annie could speak for me.

She picked up on the piqued tone of my voice and put her arm around me and kissed me on the cheek.

"We're together," she said.

Raul raised a skeptical eyebrow. "Whichever way your tastes run babe. It's your life, as they say." He went to pat a belly that wasn't there, finding only taut muscle and laughed. "Just can't get used to this new one."

"So, who else is here?" asked Annie.

"My, you have sharpened your hearing," said Raul, obviously a little taken aback. "Follow me and I shall reveal all."

We met the second immortal, Clarisse, a middle-aged woman, vastly overweight and sprouting hairs from both ruddy nostrils, in the downstairs section of a crowded Italian restaurant.

"My research has shown he likes to take the pretty ones first," said Clarisse, reacting to the shocked looks on the faces of Annie and Raul.

"And when he comes for the ugly fuckers, surely they need to be mobile enough to run away," said Raul.

"You survive your way, I'll survive mine, pretty boy. Now cut the crap and tell us why you've been spraying your mental spores through the capital's airwaves."

Immediately, I felt an affinity for Clarisse. She would not take any crap from this peacock.

"And while I'm in a moaning mood," she added, "what's the lifer doing here?"

"He's with me," said Annie.

"Figures. Come on, Raul – what do you want? I've got a date tonight."

"I'm afraid you will have to take a rain check on that. There's somebody who wants to meet you both." He tapped the side of his nose. "Very hush-hush. Very important."

Clarisse shifted her bulk as if to leave, then farted, sighed with either frustration or satisfaction, then stared down the shocked occupants of the next table. "Raul, either tell me what you want in a straightforward sentence in the next ten seconds or I'm gone."

"Duvall wants to meet with us."

Nobody spoke.

———

RAUL DROVE us out of London through the rain-slicked night. Excited chatter had replaced silence, but most of what was being said, shifting between story and speculation, was lost on me. I felt utterly extraneous to the group. Annie occasionally patted my leg or flashed what I imagined was supposed to be a reassuring grin, but neither gesture helped.

I tried to get a handle on what was happening. Duvall was a legend within the tribe. One of the oldest and bravest who had taken it upon himself to hunt down the hunter and rid them of Jeremiah. However, he hadn't been seen or heard from in many years. Rumour had it that Jeremiah had killed him in Cairo. This had never been verified.

"Why did he contact you?" asked Clarisse.

"All in good time," Raul had a self-satisfied grin on his face.

The city gave way to suburbs and then we were passing through the blackness of the countryside along unlit roads.

"Why out here?" asked Clarisse, then added in a mocking impersonation of Raul's voice, "*All in good time.*"

We turned off the main road on to a narrower track that led to an abandoned aerodrome. Annie slipped her hand into mine and squeezed. I squeezed back. She looked excited or scared, probably both. I had a sick feeling in the stomach. This wasn't right. This definitely did not feel right.

Raul drove us alongside a hangar that looked like half of an enormous barrel, then straight through the open door. Inside, the car's engine echoed loud and angry. Moonlight angled in through windows set three-quarters of the way up the curvature of the building.

"Right, everybody out," said Raul, cutting the engine. "He's up there."

He pointed at the far of the end of the hangar, where a set of steps led up to a small office. Blinds obscured the only window. A line of tungsten light sneaked out at the bottom of the door.

Clarisse clambered out of the car, sniffed the dank air and farted. Annie climbed out from the back door. I hesitated for a moment, watching Raul, who leant across the passenger seat, rummaging in the glove compartment.

"Out you get, lifer," he said, almost jovially, glancing over his shoulder. There was something off with his expression; tension pulling his facial muscles in directions that belied the tone of his voice.

I should have trusted my instincts and stayed in the car. As soon as I was out, leaving Raul alone inside, he slammed his door closed. Central locking sucked bolts into holes. The hangar cast echoes of the slamming door from wall to wall. The engine came to life. Annie and Clarisse, caught in the headlights, breath clouding, turned and stared at Raul. Small animals about to meet their unmaker.

"I'm sorry," shouted Raul from inside the car. "It's two for the price of one. It's the only way."

The car squealed into reverse, back towards the hangar doors.

"No," shouted Annie, slapping her hands to her head.

"Jeremiah," said Clarisse, her voice low and empty of inflection.

I sprinted hard after the car, racing towards the hangar doors. Raul braked once he was outside the hangar, jumped from the car, grabbed the high hangar door and started to pull it closed. I sprinted harder as the view of the night-time fields narrowed, the rusty door screaming on its rollers.

I didn't make it. The door clanged shut, sealing me inside with the others. I heard a chain rattling, a padlock snapping shut.

"Let us out, you bastard." I hammered on the door, filling the hangar with echoes of violence.

I heard the car turn on the gravel and then pull away, moving along the side of the hangar. Then it stopped. It couldn't have gone out of earshot that quickly.

A thump and a muffled scream. Annie and Clarisse were beside me now, pulling at the door. Annie kept glancing over her shoulder at the office and the thin strip of light beneath its door.

"There must be a way. Has to be," she muttered.

We worked our way around the edge of the hangar, kicking at the wall, seeking weak spots or vandalism that might aid our escape. But Raul had chosen his trap well. All

I found was a rusty old monkey wrench. I hefted it. At least I had some kind of weapon with which to protect Annie.

"You may as well have a toothpick," scoffed Clarisse, seeing the wrench.

There was no way out. We had circled the hangar, getting as close as we dared to the steps leading to the office. Annie slumped down against the wall, cradling her head, moaning.

Footsteps crunched on the gravel, approaching the hangar door.

"It's Raul," said Clarisse. "I knew the bastard couldn't do it."

I remembered the car starting to move away, then stopping. Had he had second thoughts? Then I remembered the muffled scream. The padlock dropped to the floor and the chain rattled free. Clarisse was moving towards the door. Annie followed her, but I grabbed her arm, pulling her back.

"Let go of me – it's Raul," she spat at me.

"It's not him. He's dead," I said, suddenly certain. Jeremiah wouldn't settle for two, when he could trick all three into a trap.

"No," she screamed. She was almost free of my grip. "Let go of me, lifer."

I forgave her for that. She was only speaking the truth.

The chain fell to the floor and the hangar door screamed open. The angular-faced man, Ezekiel Jeremiah, was backlit by moonlight, knife in hand. This was the way he wanted it. The executioner blessed by Mother Nature on his sacred crusade. Clarisse screamed and waddled away from her hunter, but Raul's acidic comments about her physique were true. Jeremiah caught her at a jog.

I didn't want to stay and watch. I squeezed the wrench

in one hand and with the other hauled Annie behind me. "Up the stairs."

We were almost at the top, and I could already see into the empty office when Clarisse screamed. Annie pulled her hand from mine and turned to look down at her comrade. I tried to pull her into the office, but she was gripping tightly onto the metal stair rail. I looked down. Jeremiah had cut away Clarisse's clothes and now was cutting her body open from the throat to the belly.

There are some things that cannot be forgiven.

Despite her wounds, Clarisse was fighting, thrashing in Jeremiah's grip with an inhuman frenzy, her body blurring. But she couldn't maintain her ferocity. She screamed for help.

"Joshua, help me! Joshua, please!" A weak arm reaching up towards us. Towards Annie. Pleading eyes locked with Annie's.

Joshua?

"Joshua, please don't leave me. Joshuaaaa." The last word rose to a scream as the knife plummeted towards her heart.

Joshua? Annie?

Annie closed her eyes as Clarisse died, then looked me in the eye, her expression beyond my comprehension. "Yes. Joshua," she said.

Footsteps from below, deliberate and arrogant. Jeremiah waggled the bloody knife in the moonlight and came for us.

Joshua. I pushed the name away. My mind zoned in on survival and survival alone. Simple calculations. Ignore the rest. Leave the mess and confusion and hate. Simple calculations.

The office had a window on the far wall. From this there was a drop of twenty feet to a pile of soil and tangled crop of bushes. On the road alongside the hangar was Raul's car. Jeremiah had cut him open and displayed him on the bonnet. Simple calculations. Jump from the window, risking broken limbs, but allowing a chance to reach the car. Or wait for Jeremiah and death.

I jumped, landing painfully, thorns embedding themselves into thigh and buttock, and hobbled towards the car. I heard Annie land behind me. She squealed in discomfort, but I heard her follow me. I slid Raul off the bonnet, leaving it slick with blood, and climbed into the driver's seat. I still had the wrench in my hand, as if it had now become an extra brutal limb. I rested it across my lap. The keys were still in the ignition. Too arrogant to consider anybody might escape his trap. Annie climbed into the passenger seat. I think she was talking to me. *At* me. In the corner of my eye I saw Jeremiah drop from the window, landing sweetly, rolling forward and sprinting towards the car. I turned the key in the ignition, but nothing happened. Again; nothing. Annie screaming. Jeremiah closing in. Then the sound of the engine filled the night, and we were accelerating away, our pursuer, incredibly, gaining on us for a few terrifying seconds, then diminishing in the rear-view mirror, knife thrown onto the road in disgust.

I didn't know where I was heading; all I knew was that I needed to increase the distance from the madman with the knife. Left and right down curving countryside lanes. Nobody but us in the night.

I did not look to my left. I could not look to my left. At her. At him. If I did, I wouldn't be able to hold back the deep, dammed-up waters of incomprehension. Tears of anger and self-pity blurred my vision. A hand overlaid mine on the steering wheel. I tossed it aside.

"I'm still your Annie," he said.

That was all it took to break the dam.

I slammed on the brakes, the car sliding across the road, and climbed out. I couldn't order a single thought – fear and sadness and adrenaline and all the colliding confusion. I smashed the wrench into the bonnet a dozen times and the violence seemed to help me see. How had I accepted this madness with such ease? This creature, this unnatural thing, had killed Annie, and not the slightest moral doubt had hampered my complicity. The old Annie had been right about me. I had no morals. I was shallow. I believed in nothing other than the gratification of myself. I deserved deception.

Old Annie. New Annie. Joshua. Three faces.

Joshua grabbed my arm, trying to force me to look at Annie's face. Shouting. "What's changed? I'm still the same soul in the same skin. A name means nothing."

"You lied to me," and my shout was like a roar. I hammered the bonnet again. "You're a man."

"It's just a name."

"It's a sex. It's your history. Your life, you lying fucking bastard." I raised the wrench above my head and lunged towards him. He did not back away. She did not back away. The wrench hung above me, my frustration so great I could barely see.

"I'm a person," he said.

"You're a man."

"So what? Sex is just meat."

The wrench came down, catching him above the ear, knocking him to the ground, bleeding and gasping on all fours. The second strike heralded the crack and collapse of his skull.

I'M A MURDERER. This is me. He's dead now. She's dead now. Both of them. I succeeded where Jeremiah failed.

(His fingers are still in her hair, gently touching the fragments of bone. He had wanted to destroy this human cockpit where the devious soul lived. His stomach convulses. He feels distant from his body. Nausea descends.)

Why did I have to hate?

(He shakes his head, scattering tears. Then he hears another voice within himself. *You let it nest in you*, says the voice.)

I didn't choose. I never had the choice. I wouldn't have chosen hate.

(His nausea has receded, but he feels more distant from his body. As if his violence has set him adrift. *You let it breed*, says the voice.)

I couldn't. I didn't know how.

(And now he can feel the presence inside him. Realises it has been there ever since he killed Joshua. He looks at the dead body on the road. The empty shell.)

Joshua?

(*Yes, Joshua.*)

You can't take me.

(*Hate always leads to true sadness, it is too great a burden for any mortal. I am saving you. I love you too much to let you live a sad life.*)

No.

(He drifts away from his body, seeing it stand before the corpse and drop the wrench. Then he is drifting apart. He is gone. He is safe.)

"*We only take the sad*," says Joshua, stretching his arms, wearing his new skin.

KISSED BY THE MOTH

The sash window was old and accommodating. The frames parted without complaint as the thief inserted a chisel and slowly pushed the rusty swing lock up and out of its rotten anchorage. Sultry night air clambered into the room with him. He breathed in the flat's scents: garlic, lemon polish, perfume, the tang of cigarettes. Static tingled in his palm as he stroked the nap of the velvet sofa. In the bedroom, a man and woman lay in a tangle of sweaty sheets. The woman's left leg was uncovered, lightly tanned and distinct against the white sheets. The thief held out a hand an inch above the silky sweep of flesh. He watched the sheets rise and fall. After a while he took what he came for. The man and woman did not stir.

When the man woke, he eased himself out of bed, pulled on shorts and a T-shirt and tiptoed into the kitchen. Put on a pot of coffee. Picked up shards of a broken wine-glass; a result of last night's argument. He stared out of the kitchen window, mind blank. The percolator gurgled, and he carried a steaming mug and his cigarettes into the small garden. The parched yellow grass, sprouting between the cracks in the paving, was a victim of the vicious heatwave choking the city. He sat down and plucked a few pathetic blades.

Dying in the heat, he thought. *Just like our relationship.* Quickly, he chided himself for being so childish and melodramatic – a blazing argument does not the end of a relationship make. He looked at the bedroom window. The curtains were still closed. *Should I wake her? No. Let things take their natural course. When she's ready, she'll wake. When we're ready, we'll talk. When we've talked, we'll make up – then things can carry on as they should.*

He lit a cigarette and sipped his coffee. Absently, he scratched at itches on his chest and neck. Red welts prickled into life on his skin. Had she scratched him when they fought? He didn't remember that. Maybe it was the ants. He watched platoons of them scurrying in and out of the cracks in the paving and flicked the occasional boulder of ash onto them. He chuckled to himself – insect Pompeii.

When she came to the kitchen door, arms folded and clutching her silk dressing gown, she had tears on her pillow-creased cheeks. *This isn't the natural course of things*, he thought. Silent reproof was the natural course.

We've been burgled, she told him.

He sat staring at her. Too much wine last night. His mind felt so slow. He checked the word against his mental inventories of sarcasm and humour and he realised she was being serious.

He followed her through to the living room. A gentle breeze was blowing through the jimmied window and lifting the net curtain into the air. A passerby looked into the room and then walked on.

The man went to comfort the woman, then hesitated, unsure what to do in the circumstances. The woman flinched as if his hesitation was a slap. In silence, they checked to see what the thief had taken. There was nothing missing.

Later, the police officer agreed that it was rare for a burglar to leave empty-handed, but ventured that the intruder must have sensed their sleeping presence and played safe. According to the officer, most thieves were cowards. Wearily, he noted down a few details and gave them a number to ring in case they discovered anything amiss. He wiped his sweaty pate with a handkerchief and left. The man felt sorry for the officer. His stomach was spilling over his belt and between the buttons at the bottom of his shirt. He looked like he was melting in the midday sun.

The forensics officer who came to dust for prints agreed that it was strange that the intruder left empty-handed. He took nothing and left nothing, the officer concluded quickly, giving up on finding any usable prints. He packed away his brush and powdered aluminium and left.

The woman ran a hand through her hair, easing out knots. The man creased a smile onto his face. *So it wasn't a thief, it was an intruder*, he thought, but said nothing.

When they were alone, the woman said that she didn't want to stay inside the house. It didn't feel clean. She put on shorts and a white vest top and took a pile of magazines out to the garden. The man dampened a cloth and wiped away the fingerprint powder staining the windowsill: rosin, black ferric oxide, lampblack. It looked like powder from a moth's wing.

He watched people walk past the window and wondered if any of these smiling, chatting, sweaty faces belonged to the intruder. What would he have done if he'd caught somebody climbing through the window? Grabbed him and called the police? Kicked the shit out of him? Which course of action would cause her to love him more? He really wasn't sure. He spied on her through the kitchen window, one arm braced behind her head, looking at the sun through thick, dark sunglasses. She was scratching her chest, leaving red marks on her breastbone. *Definitely ants*, he thought. She'd removed her shorts to allow the maximum amount of sun to her legs.

They were due to be flying out to Cyprus for a holiday in a week's time, but now? He considered asking her if she wanted an iced drink, but fixed only one for himself and shuffled back into the living room.

Time to do something about the window. He fished out a replacement lock from his bits-and -bobs drawer and looked at the lock. The intruder had forced the bottom half free of the window frame, but the top half remained in place. He had known he would regret painting over the lock last summer. He scraped paint away from the head of the screw, slipped the screwdriver into the depressed cross and pushed and twisted at the same time.

Damn: a creak, but no give. Sweat ran into his eyes and down the side of his ribcage. He pulled his T-shirt over his head and cursed again.

What's the problem? She leant against the door frame, looking at him with conciliatory eyes. There was a hint of a smile at the corners of her mouth.

In the normal course of things, this would have been more than enough. He would have dropped the screwdriver and hugged her. Promised never to argue with her again. But not today. The lock and screws were still between them. If he could remove the lock, he could remove the intruder, and then things would flow as they should.

No problem, he said to her, twisting screwdriver and

sinew and finally feeling the screw squeak free of the paint. As he turned to grin at her, the screwdriver head slipped free and plowed across his palm. For a second the slit line of flesh was clean, then it turned red and his palm filled with blood.

She was at his side.

I'm sorry, he said.

So am I, she said. She looked at his bloody hand and then pressed the bottom of her T-shirt against the wound. It didn't stop the blood flow. Her eyes met his, and she raised his hand, pressing it against her left breast. She kissed him as the blood soaked into the vest. He could feel her nipple swell against his wound. A bright calming light filed his mind. She was at its centre.

Come on, she said, holding him close and leading him to the bedroom. The front of her vest was red. He helped her pull it over her head. The welts on his chest and neck were stinging. They lay down on the bed and he put his wounded hand between her legs. She sighed as they stretched against each other. Their blood-slicked chests slid against each other. They gripped each other tight. Whispered their love.

He opened his eyes. When he pulled away, she put her hands to his cheeks and asked him was what the matter. He pointed to the bloody knife on the pillow. She screamed and jerked upright. The white sheets were now a red pool around them. She saw him shake his head as he fingered the knife wounds on his neck and chest. She felt her own pain. Now they knew what the thief had taken. Tearfully, they embraced each other and let things take their natural course.

THE MICE OF XANTITHE

__Stay in a refurbished Venetian townhouse – get__
__close to the island's unique history...__
(© Our Different Planet: Travel Guide to Xantithe 2016)

When I check into my hotel in the centre of town – a beautifully resorted, Venetian merchant's house – I'm greeted by the owner, Georgios, a large, middle-aged man with a crown of curly white hair and a black shirt. His torso is covered by a pelt of curly white hair too. A puckered, faded scar runs across his forehead.

"Taxi good?" he says, handing over my room keys.

I nod. "Very good. Very... *fast*. The driver said he was your cousin."

"Everybody in Xantithe is my cousin," says Georgios, throwing his arms wide, as if to hug the crumbling town that the taxi had shot through as if the driver was auditioning for a remake of *Bullitt*.

"Anyway," he says, "welcome back."

I smile. Shake my head. "This is my first time here."

"No," says Georgios. "I never forget a pretty lady. You have stayed before. Maybe twice."

I shake my head. "First time."

A door creaks open behind me and the back of my scalp tickles as if somebody has run a hand through my hair. Georgios frowns. When I turn, the door is already closing. I glimpse the hem of a short, red dress and a slender, tanned leg sporting an ankle bracelet.

"Mice," says Georgios, making the sign of the cross above his chest and kissing his knuckle.

"Mice?"

"Mice," he repeats, more forcefully. And as he exits by a door behind the counter: "Don't bring them under my roof."

A strange man.

After unpacking and a quick shower, I head out to explore the old town. An Orthodox priest glowers at me from beneath bushy eyebrows, probably thinking my shorts indecently short, or my long legs startlingly white, as I stroll down a steep winding street towards the harbour. Balconies cling to whitewashed walls above the narrow thoroughfare. Flowers twist through the wrought iron and dangle down like garlands, casting arabesque shadows below. Cats laze in the shade. The smell of aniseed, freshly-made bread and oleander hang in the air. A group of old men playing a game that looks like backgammon, but with a circular board, watch me pass from the porch of a kafenio Their heads move as one. Worry beads rattle as they're twirled around fingers. I nod a hello and they nod back in reply. I move on. Behind me, I hear laughter and counters slapping onto the board.

I get lost. Double back. I can't find the old men. Lines of washing hang limp above me. The sun hammers down. I'm sweating. My T-shirt sticks to my back and breasts.

Eventually, I find my way through the maze and the harbour opens up in front of me. Dusk is falling and rose-petal light caresses the crumbling Venetian buildings now occupied by restaurants and kafenia A turtle raises its gnarled head above the harbour's pewter-coloured water, flares its nostrils and slides back out of sight. The sunset tessellates on the water. I order an ouzo and sit watching the world pass. Tourists and locals, all caught up in their rituals. A pretty girl passes me. She's wearing a short red dress, but no ankle bracelet. She catches me watching her and smiles. I turn away and sip my ouzo, feeling my face flush. A couple of locals at the next table laugh. I don't know if they are laughing at me.

I leave, forgetting to pay, and the waitresses chases me along the harbour. I apologise profusely and tip her €5. She looks at me like I'm a crazy woman.

In a square two streets back from the harbour, there is a statue of a man with his arm stuck up a horse's anus. Not an auspicious pose, you might think, but I had read all about this famous sculpture. Locally, it's known as *The Horse That Ate the Turk*. It dates back to the attempted Ottoman invasion of the island in 1643. The Greek freedom fighters, led by their ruthless leader, called *The Mountain's Fang*, had abandoned the capital. Such had been the speed of the Ottoman advance, it had been a disorderly retreat to their mountain fastness, and they had been forced to leave a huge cache of weapons in a cellar beneath the Byzantine monastery of St. Emilia. The monastery's bishop, a veritable warrior of the Orthodox church, hid the key to the cellar key deep inside his favourite mare's rectum.

The Ottomans tore the monastery to pieces looking for the key. When they couldn't find it, they tortured the bishop. Sheltered by prayer and armoured by faith, the bishop withstood every cut and tear until his body gave out and he made his ascent to heaven. In a savage rage, the Ottoman commander ordered his troops to blast their way into the cellar. An officer urged caution – the rebels might have stored gunpowder inside, he argued. The officer lost his head (literally) and his replacement hastily stacked explosives against the cellar and lit the gunpowder trail.

Three hundred and fifty Ottoman soldiers perished in the resulting explosion. The invasion faltered and within days the army set sail for easier conquests. Sadly, the monastery, with its majestic Byzantine frescoes, was lost for all time. After the invasion, one of the surviving priests rescued the key from its anal hiding place and the entire town knelt before it. To this day, the key hangs around the neck of the town priest.

"It never happened." A voice at my side.

The woman was in her mid-twenties. Long ebony hair, olive skin, eyes the colour of polished cedar.

"Excuse me?"

"They didn't hide the key up the horse's arse."

I nod. She's wearing a red dress. A slender bracelet circles her ankle.

Mice.

"The bishop, who was a big man, hid it up his own arse."

"No?"

"Yes. Not a statue the church would ever commission." She bends over, pushing out her bottom. Her dress rides up her thighs. "Lacks the necessary heroism, no?"

"Indeed."

"Do you want a tour of the town?" she says, straightening up.

"Sounds lovely. Are you Georgios' daughter? From the hotel?" I wave a hand back towards the old town.

The woman laughs and shakes her head. Not a *no* shake of the head, more a *what is this foreigner like?* shake of the head.

"Follow me. I know a good place for dinner," she says.

***

The local cuisine truly is the food of the gods...
(© Our Different Planet: Travel Guide to Xantithe 2016)

SHE WEAVES a complex route through the labyrinthine old town and arrives at an open-roofed building cleverly frozen at a point of designer decrepitude. The high walls are artfully crumbling but appear secure. Vines climb the stones and then wind themselves around virtually invisible wires that cross the space. Bundles of young grapes hang down. The air smells of wild oregano and candles scented with a rich perfume. There's a headless statue of a woman in robes baring her left breast. A fountain burbles at the centre of the dining space, tables arrayed around it. Above, large lanterns cast complex patterns across diners and tables. The total effect is magical.

"Sit," says the woman. She's already sitting at a table, a handsome, bearded young waiter at her side. His arms are deeply tanned and corded with muscles and tattoos.

"It's lovely," I say, sitting.

She ignores me and rattles out a command in Greek. The waiter wrinkles his brow and asks a question. She repeats herself slowly, more forcefully, and he bows deferentially. I use the distraction to study her. The lantern above our table turns slowly in the gentlest of breezes, its shadows caressing her features: high cheek bones, kohl-outlined eyes with hazel irises, full lips with an imperious twist, a necklace of intertwining loops plummeting towards the scooped neckline of her dress, where gem-like beads of sweat glitter.

"What are you looking at?" she says, as the waiter hurries away.

"Your necklace," I say.

"I think you're lying."

"Oh." I don't know what to say.

"You were looking at my breasts."

"I... errr."

"Do you think my breasts would look like the goddess Malera's?" she says, nodding at the statue.

"I hadn't really studied them," I say, then add quickly: "I mean Malera's breasts, not yours. I'm digging a hole, aren't I? I'm sure your breasts are equally divine as Malera's."

At this pun, her face relaxes into a not entirely comforting smile and I take a breath I hadn't realised I'd been denying myself.

"I'm only teasing," she says, as the waiter returns and sets little glasses of amber liquid before us. "How did you become so English?" she says.

"I've always been like this."

"I don't think so."

"Well, I must have practiced very hard," I say, shrugging, which elicits another of those smiles.

"Yes, you must."

"I've never heard of the goddess Malera," I say, trying to change the subject, but feeling lightheaded and suddenly unsure of myself.

"She is unique to Xantithe. As are many of our customs, foods and drinks," she says, raising her glass, closing one eye and peering at me with the other through the amber liquid. "Like the Goddess' Tears. The perfect drink to – how should I say it in English? – re-attune you to my island."

I follow her lead, tipping back my head and swallowing the shot of spirit in one burning slug. It races down my throat, setting fire to my nerves and exploding outwards through my body to the tip of every limb. In my mind's eye, I imagine my head splitting into fragments, shuffling in the air above my headless torso and reforming as an unfamiliar person. Suddenly, I feel voraciously hungry. I'm sweating. I try to refocus on her through tearful eyes.

"Jesus, that's strong," I say, as the room concertinas in and out around me.

"That charlatan has nothing to do with anything," she says, and then the evening really gets weird.

You'll find the locals welcoming and warm ...
(© Our Different Planet: Travel Guide to Xantithe 2016)

I WAKE NAKED, sprawled across the bed in the hotel. I try to raise my head, but sharp pain jags through it at multiple angles. I lower it to the pillow.

Memories strobe in my mind: the woman.

Oh my God, what have I done? I flop out an arm, reaching out, pat the bed.

"Hello?"

No answer. I'm alone.

I try to move again, but the pain is too intense. I moan and dig into my tender mind. My memories are like a freshly unearthed ancient mural: fragmentary, faded, incorrectly reconfigured, broken; the woman above me (*what is her name?*), long hair hanging down and brushing my face and breasts, sweat dripping from her face, and then she's looking up at me from between my legs saying *remember me*; diners chased from the restaurant, scared expressions as they pushed and bumped their way to the street beyond, casting glances over their shoulders; shelves of bowls, coins, spears, swords, life-sized statues complete, decapitated and limbless, an exhibit at the centre of a museum, six artfully lit sculpted heads, a live mouse sitting atop one; I'm drinking more shots of the Goddess' Tears, new people in the restaurant with us, we're sitting in a circle, they're staring at me and firing off questions, laughing, swearing, taunting; the streets reeling around me, emptying of people, doors and shutters hurriedly closing as we pass; her body clothed only in shadows, sashaying towards me.

I force myself to rise and stagger to the bathroom. I swallow painkillers, washing them down with tap water. I open my eyes. They stare back at me pink, squinting. I have bite marks on my breasts. I touch them and another memory flashes: bright, hot sunshine, stone pillars, somebody drawing symbols on my body with a finger dipped in a bowl of thick ruby fluid.

How did this happen? I've never had sex with a woman

before. Fantasies, yes, but I've fantasised about lots of things. I realise that despite the horrendous hangover I feel good; I feel alive, warm inside.

I dress and stagger down to the breakfast room. The smell of coffee and warm bread greets me. I'm ravenous again. I spread honey on bread, wolf down cheese and meat, guzzle orange juice and coffee. Georgios enters the room and approaches me, unsmiling. He hands me a leaflet: *THE ARCHEOLOGICAL MUSEUM OF XANTITHE.*

"You should go here today," he says and leaves the room. "Then find another hotel."

"What? I…"

He's already gone. The other guests are staring at me as if I might be trouble. I turn the leaflet over. It carries two grainy images of headless statues and a badly translated block of text: *Enjoy this ecseptional collection of relixs and…*

I stop reading. The sculptures; I remember the sculptures. Was I in the museum last night? There was a mouse, a live mouse sitting on the top of a sculpture of a woman's head. That must have been a dream, but… I remember something else and I'm suddenly cold, confused, uncertain. I stand too quickly and the legs of my table scrape against the floor. Diners whisper as I hurry from the room.

Xantithe is home to a number of excellent museums…

(© Our Different Planet: Travel Guide to Xantithe 2016)

THE MUSEUM HASN'T YET OPENED when I arrive. I knock on the door, hoping somebody will let me in early, but there is no response other than the echo of knuckles on wood. I kill an hour in a kafenio across the road. I sip a coffee and eat a slab of baklava and ice cream. Where did my appetite come from? I use my phone to browse the internet for information on the goddess Malera. My feet tap the warming pavement nervously. There is surprisingly little information online, and what there is hotly contested. Some claim that Malera is nothing more than an elaborate hoax; ancient fake news.

Eventually, I find a PDF of an old doctoral thesis which references six gods unique to the island of Xantithe. Gods that avoided the extinction of Zeus and his cohorts heralded by the arrival of the Christians, by turning themselves into mice and continuing to live in the world of men.

Mice. Goddesses and gods.

The museum opens and I hurry inside. The attendant grumbles at having to serve a customer as soon as the doors open. "I've not even had time to buy a frappe," he mutters. I push a ten-euro note at him and don't wait for my change.

The museum comprises only three rooms. The first is dedicated to pottery, the second weapons, the third sculptures. I find the six sculpted heads. There is no mouse. I read the names beneath each of the sculptures: Xantith, Quodith, Hermaxis, Allathymnin, Malera.

I stop at Malera. Stare at the beautiful face with oval eyes and full, imperious lips. It's her; it's the woman in the red dress.

"Look at the last sculpture," she says, standing close enough behind me for me to feel her breath against my neck, the warmth emanating from her body. I hadn't heard a single footstep of her approach. But then I see four white mice dashing across the room towards us and I understand.

"Look," she says again, this time more harshly, her hand warm but strong, forcing me to face the final sculpture.

I look, even though I do not need to. I saw it last night. When I saw the sculpted head, it was like looking at my reflection. I read the name below the head: Helentia.

She kisses my neck and I'm in free fall. "See? You've come back to us, my love."

The mice have disappeared. Now three men and a woman form a semicircle before me. They're all dressed in contemporary clothes but possess the same otherworldly charisma as Malera. Their gaze is a singular thing, strong, imploring

I shake my head, gritting my teeth. Slip free of her grip and run, shouting as I approach the exit, "It's not me!"

I'm out into the streets, the sun already heavy and hot, pressing down onto the city. There is no wind. Shutters screech as shops open for business. I smell leather and herbs. I weave between groups of shuffling tourists, slack-faced zombies compared to the burning presences I left behind in the museum.

But they are no longer there. I see Xantith and Quodith sitting at a cafe table watching me pass. Hermaxis looks down from the open roof deck of a city sightseeing bus. Allathymnin walks towards me arm-in-arm with two giggling Swedish tourists.

I make it back to the hotel, pay Georgios and tell him to order a taxi to the airport, *now*. Malera is waiting in my room.

"Don't go, again," she says, trying to embrace me. I shrug her off and stuff clothes into my suitcase.

"I love you," she says. "I need you."

I ignore her, checking my travel documents, calculating the price I will have to pay to change my flight date.

"You promised to only go out amongst the cattle for a year. It's been ten years now. You leave, forget everything that has happened as soon as you set foot on the plane, then return the following year and we play out this charade. Why do you refuse to remember us? You belong here. This island will draw you back like a magnet for eternity. My love will draw you back."

She wraps her arms tight around me and kisses my neck again. I shudder, my will folding memories into strange shapes.

"Sorry, my love, but this time it has to be different. My heart cannot withstand this pain again," says Malera, then whispers words alien but familiar. She disappears and I glimpse a scurrying white ball slip into a hole in the wall.

I hurry from the room. The taxi is waiting, and the driver speeds through the city with the same abandon as my arrival transfer. There is space on the next flight. It leaves in thirty minutes. I pay the charge to change my ticket and I am rushed through security. I ride a bus alone to the plane, board and sit next to an elderly woman who smiles at me. The boarding stairs are wheeled away and the engines come to life.

I lean back into my seat, breathing deeply. The plane taxis and the engine pitch climbs. Already my memories of Malera and the others are fading. I'm changing into that other woman. The one who arrived innocent and empty of the ages. I'm asking myself a question: *Why are you leaving this lovely island early? You really need a holiday.*

Then I hear whispered words in a long-dead language and a torrential rush of memories flow into my head, obliterating the other woman.

When the old woman next to me screams, I look up at her, surprised. She stares down at me from on high.

"Attendant!" she screams. "A mouse! There's a mouse on the flight!"

You'll find yourself coming back to Xantithe time after time...
(© Our Different Planet: Travel Guide to Xantithe 2016)

AMERICAN SEXUAL LOBSTER

I was sweating. I didn't want to do it. All thoughts of kitchen kudos and higher hourly rates, all my declarations of brutal competence, had melted away. I leant my head against the cool wall. My mind hadn't recovered from the night before. What to do? Lucy emerged from the toilet, smoothing her waitress skirt over her hips. She stood inches from me, examining my face. I pushed myself upright, smiling, trying to look comfortable with the proximity of her body. She deadpanned some comment about my enduring lack of a tan (*we should call you the White Clifford of Dover*) and asked me if I'd be at the beach party that evening. I said probably. See you there, she said. And good luck with the erm... she mimed a cutting motion, winked, picked up a tray of salt cellars and athletically spun through swing doors into the restaurant.

Hey, come on, Cliffy boy. Leave the ladies till after work, man. It was Charlie, laughing through the kitchen door's fly grill. He squinted into the blaze of a beautiful Cape Cod afternoon and took a last pull on his joint. School time, he said, exhaling smoke and flicking the roach over the wall. He came inside and pulled open the door to the walk-in freezer.

The freezer shelves were crammed with trays of shell-fish: clams, oysters and mussels; jars of pickled herring; half a small shark on ice. Charlie bent over and lifted the lid of a gigantic polystyrene box. I sucked my teeth as it squeaked.

Hey, my friends, said Charlie.

And there they were – his friends, the lobsters – inside the box. Mottled red and black. About a two dozen of them, making pointless little walking motions through their bed of ice cubes. Charlie grabbed a lobster and waggled it in front of my face.

Fuck off, I shouted, jumping backwards and whacking my head on the door frame. Charlie laughed and said something about the English all being crazy. I told him to get a life and his grin slipped into a petulant scowl.

In the kitchen Charlie slapped the lobster onto its back and thrust a sharp, heavy cook's knife into my hand. Charlie wasn't interested in my conciliatory jokes, so I left him to his mood. I concentrated on the lobster. Its underside was a tight, glistening, off-white membrane with pink ridges running across it at centimetre intervals. It flexed its muscles, rolling up its armour-plated tail to protect its underside. Its tail ended in an intricate fan-like arrangement of bone. Charlie told me to get a grip of its body.

Reluctantly, I reached out and pressed down on the lobster's body with my left hand. Its underside flexed rhyth-mically, powerful muscles pressing against my palm. My scalp tingled with revulsion. The lobster didn't enjoy being manhandled; it pulled up its tail, slapping the back of my hand and curling its legs to scrape them across my skin. My stomach churned slowly. I desperately wanted to pull my hand away, but I couldn't; not in front of Charlie. Not after

I had bragged incessantly about my ability to butcher any of God's creatures without a qualm.

What now? Do I lop off its head? I asked Charlie, trying to sound brutally jovial. He must have sensed my discomfort because he hesitated, let the moment stretch out, time measured by the slap of the lobster's tail against my hand.

Stab it in the brain and cut straight down the middle of its body, he said, finally releasing me. I didn't need any encouragement. I thrust the point of the knife into the lobster. It convulsed beneath my hand, rapidly curling and uncurling its tail, crunching its muscles. Angling the knife, I leant forward and felt the blade cut through the tough membrane and then slice into the softer flesh beneath. My senses lurched as the lobster continued to writhe. Halfway down the body the knife snagged on one of the flexible pink ridges and so I shifted position and pressed down with sinew-stretching pressure. The ridge gave way, and I split the lobster from head to tail. I let out a breath and watched stars spangle in my vision. I pulled my hand away from the lobster. It didn't move.

Charlie slapped me on the back and said Well done. A broadside of a grin signaled the end of his mood. I was glad. It helped to settle my nerves a little. He took control of the lobster, showing me how to snap open the shell and remove the tiny blue intestines and slick grey brain with a dexterous sweep of two fingers and then fill the resulting cavity with seafood stuffing.

We took a break sitting on the wall out back, smoking cigarettes and watching beautiful tanned bodies strut around the beautiful white yachts moored in the harbour. Charlie speculated about the sexual athleticism of various waitresses – joking about my obvious interest in Lucy – but my sex drive was on hold. All I could think about were lobsters and the murderous night that lay ahead. I imagined thousands of them doing their strange tiptoe walk beneath the boats in the harbour, flexing their powerful bodies against the Atlantic sway and waiting. Just gazing up towards the glittering kaleidoscope of the surface, waiting.

The evening began quietly. Waitresses ambled into the kitchen bitching about pensioners changing their orders a dozen times – *No, miss, I think I will have the key lime pie* – and then sashayed back to their tables wearing their best tip-grabbing smiles. The kitchen staff goofed around, telling jokes and slurping down bowls of clam chowder. We finished all the preparations. Anxiously, I fingered my knife, trying to lose myself in the banter.

Then, suddenly, the orders built up and the atmosphere changed. Steam separated the kitchen into separate kingdoms. Each cook became a dictator, all bulging eyes, sweaty brows and tics, barking orders and curses that swirled around the kitchen on oven thermals.

Charlie called for lobster after lobster and they all fell to my knife. The routine became everything; the seal popping as I opened the freezer door, the arbitrary selection of victim, each one staring at me with stalk-like eyes, my stomach turning as it writhed in my grip like a ball of armoured muscle.

After an hour, somebody covered for me so I could take a ten-minute break. I attacked a swordfish steak with shaking hands, thinking it might help settle my stomach, but it had the opposite effect. I leant out the kitchen door, heaved up chunks of fish and returned to my station.

Feel better? asked my cover.

Sure, I lied, fumbling to pick up my knife. An hour later, the head cook barked out an order for two lobsters and I croaked that we were down to our last one.

Why the fuck didn't you tell me? he bellowed, peering wild-eyed through coils of steam. But now the kitchen frenzy had lost all power to affect me. I was numb. Sick with revulsion. Cutting up lobsters like an automaton. The palms of my hands, scraped raw by lobster shells, pulsed to the rhythm of their muscular undersides. As I snapped open the final lobster, I felt a dull frisson of release. It was over. Wild horses wouldn't drag me back to the restaurant the next day.

When the last order had been shuttled out of the kitchen by a weary waitress, we cleaned up. Charlie pressed a blissfully icy bottle of beer into my hands. I rubbed it back and forth between my palms, trying to numb the pulsing sensations. He told me it was always hardest on the first night and downed his bottle of beer in one long gulp, crowning the achievement with a fanfare of a belch. I downed half my bottle. It felt good. I finished the rest, and the brew weaved its way towards my stomach, cooling my queasy innards and soothing my nerves. I threw the empty into a trashcan.

Something crawled about inside the trashcan, as if disturbed by the bottle. It was my trashcan, the one I had been gradually filling as the night progressed. I turned to Charlie, but he had disappeared into the restaurant. The crawling noise stopped. I kicked the trashcan: nothing. Carefully, I lifted it, carried it at arms' length and dumped it into the huge cylindrical bins at the back of the restaurant. When I pressed my ear to the metal, I could hear movement inside. Something shuffling through the scraps and offal. I hurried back into the restaurant, washed myself in icy water and changed. The others were waiting for me and we wandered down to the beach.

As soon as I saw the sea, I started to scratch my palms,

trying to rid them of the memory of the rhythmic motions of the lobsters, but it only had the effect of reawakening the sensations. I looked around for help, or at least distraction. In the distance, I could see the yachts in the harbour with strings of light draped from mast to prow and stern. All I could think of was what lurked below them, tiptoeing through the black ocean. Then something pulled me back to the beach. A physical sensation – Lucy tickling me. In a burst of sand, she was up and running down the beach, laughing and waving a bottle of beer. Charlie shadowed her, shouting out football calls and threatening to tackle her. I grabbed a bottle from a crate and downed half of it.

For an hour I tried to get drunk, tipping an endless golden stream down my throat, but it had all the effect of a gallon of Dr Pepper; I felt bloated with gas, ready to puke again. Music thumped the night sky and people danced around blazing tin drums and barbecues, laughing and groping, but I was apart from it all, once-removed in a state of heightened awareness that refused to be dulled by anything as simple as alcohol. I could see what others couldn't. Something, or some things, were moving about in the moonlit surf. Careful to keep just out of my sight, they scuttled in and out with the rhythm of the waves, although occasionally they weren't quick enough and I would glimpse shell or claw.

Lucy dropped to the sand beside me, panting. There was a smudge of charcoal on her left cheek. She grabbed my beer with a sandy hand and took a deep swallow.

Why aren't you playing? she asked.

I said I was tired after my first night of mass murder.

She laughed. Don't be a girl, she said, leaning forward and kissing me on the lips. The kiss lingered, and I rested my hand on her waist. She pushed her body against mine, opened her mouth wider and sighed. We lay down on the sand together. My eyes were closed, but I was still seeing the edge of the ocean in my mind. Movement in the breaking surf. Something emerging. I had to fight an overwhelming desire to pull away from Lucy and reassure myself that they weren't crawling towards us through the sand.

Lucy must have sensed my distraction because she pushed her body against me urgently, demanding attention, concentration. I slipped my hand under her T-shirt and stroked her smooth, muscular stomach. She moaned and bit my lip. I felt her muscles contract against my palm. The sensation sent a wave of revulsion through my body. Rhythmic, muscular movements. I imagined raised pink ridges across her stomach.

I yanked myself away from Lucy and staggered to my feet. I was shaking violently. She shouted something at me, but in my confusion I lost the meaning of the words. People were staring at us. I turned and sprinted straight into the surf, screaming and kicking at the waves, punching the pewter foam.

And then all the other partygoers were joining me in the surf, laughing and splashing each other. Pushing each other under the waves. They didn't understand. I screamed at them that this wasn't a game, they needed to get out, but nobody listened. Then Lucy was in front of me. Grabbing my arms and shouting at me. I pushed her away and she staggered back onto the beach. I refocused my anger on the water, pummelling and stamping, losing myself in a fountain of spray.

I don't know how long I spent attacking the surf, but when I next looked up I was alone, soaked to the skin and shivering. I wandered onto the beach. The tin-drum fires were nearly out, a few coals glowing like red eyes, releasing tiny curls of smoke.

I knew now that I couldn't fight them. I'd have to atone for what I had done. I wandered back to the restaurant and climbed over a wall into the yard where the large trashcans were kept. Setting my shoulder against one, I bent low to lever it forward and I pushed it up and over. It clanged like a bell. The smell of fish and rotten vegetables clung to me as I climbed into its orifice and dragged the trash into the open. Holding my breath, I sorted out every piece of lobster shell that I could find, placing them in a neat pile alongside me.

When I was sure that my collection would suffice, I put it into plastic bags and ran back down to the beach. Moonlight stretched like a silver path from beach to horizon. I tipped the contents of my bags onto the sand at the edge of the ocean and stripped off my clothes. I lobbed them into the sea and watched the tide carry them out.

Then, carefully, using a little sea water as adhesive, I stuck the pieces of lobster shell onto my body. First my face, then my arms, legs and back as best as I could. I left my belly open to the air.

I breathed the sea air deeply and waded into the water. They were still hidden from me, but I knew they were there, waiting in judgement in the deep waters – looking up to the surface from amongst the rocks and kelp. Standing on their tiptoes. Waiting.

The shells soon slipped from my body, but it didn't matter. I had made my gesture. I was swimming as fast as I could, heading out to the deep water. My limbs soon tired, but I couldn't stop yet. A spasm of cramp straightened my right leg and seawater lapped into my mouth. I tried to bend my foot and relieve the pain, but it was difficult to do while treading water with one leg.

When cramp struck my left leg, I knew I was finished. I took a last look at the moon. As I slipped under the surface, I could see it ripple on the surface. I tried to peer down to the dark depths, but my eyes were nothing but a stinging blur. As water filled my lungs, I prayed for forgiveness.

THE ANATOMY OF TEARS

Isabel Lacombe pulled on the white hospital gown. Then, as instructed, she cleansed her face of all makeup using the bottled fluids provided, paying particular attention to the skin around her eyes and cheeks. She smiled approvingly at her unadorned face, not out of vanity, but professional pride. As an actress, she took care of the tools of her trade.

"Can you cry for me?" said Dr Celeste.

"I can," said Isabel.

"Please do so," he said.

Isabel was now seated on a chair in a glaring-white sterile room. It was silent except for the low hum of an air filter and the scraping of metal instruments as Dr Celeste prepared for the experiment.

"Now?" she asked.

"Now, please."

Dr Celeste reduced the level of light in the room. A green bulb glowed on the box, suspended by a hydraulic arm 30 centimetres from Isabel's face. He placed his head next to the box and adjusted its position a fraction.

Only the band of flesh around Dr Celeste's eyes was

visible. A green surgical mask and cap covered the rest of his head. His eyes fascinated Isabel; scientific eyes; kaleidoscopic blues sharp enough to slice diamonds.

"If you find that you are not able to cry under these circumstances, I will understand," said Dr Celeste.

Isabel savoured his eyes for a few more seconds: "I'm always able to cry." She flicked the switch of her acting method, flooding her mind with memories of her mother dying in a hospital bed; the noise she had made in her throat; monstrous delusions and accusations. It was the most powerful stimulus she had at her command. Her face collapsed and tears ran into the creases below her eyes. A sob caught in her throat.

A wide beam of light scrolled down her face and cheeks, mapping tears and trajectories. At the side of the room, a computer screen created lines of data. Isabel felt glass against her cheek as Dr Celeste harvested tears and placed them into a storage device.

"Thank you," said Dr Celeste. He handed Isabel a paper tissue and raised the level of light in the room. "Would you like to lie down for a while?"

"No, I'm fine, thank you," said Isabel.

Isabel was doubly thrilled by Dr Celeste's invitation to take part in his research. It wasn't often that she worked with people of renown outside the arts. Some even whispered the word *genius* when mentioning Celeste's name. An added attraction to the man's stellar professional reputation was his cool sexual presence and her suspicions that his invitation concealed a personal agenda. She could feel the hunger in his gaze.

"Why did you insist that my involvement in your research be kept secret, Pascal?" He hadn't invited her to call him Pascal, but she prided herself on being able to read people's tolerances.

Dr Celeste ignored her question and continued to tap at a keyboard, eyes flicking between a monitor and the glass cabinet in front of him. Ice climbed across the glass from each of its corners. He had told her he was freezing her tears into a sheet that was only a few molecules thick.

"The same strictures have applied to each of the nine other women who have participated in the research," he said.

Isabel smarted at the words. She hoped that she had been his first and only choice.

"Some may consider my current work to be of a... dubious nature. I don't wish to court any attention at this point in time."

"And yet you let me watch the process."

"I let you watch the process because you are here and you asked." His eyes settled on her again. It felt like they were opening her, entering her. She shifted in her seat. "Nobody else has witnessed the process. You are the first. You are also the first person *not* to ask for a fee."

Isabel smiled at this.

"And what secret is the process designed to reveal?" she asked. "I may as well be the first to know that too."

Dr Celeste didn't miss a beat. "I'm searching for the image of emotion in the heart of tears."

The image of emotion in the heart of tears. Isabel caressed the words in her mind; science dancing with poetry. A sensual surge of elation rippled through her body. The man was a poet.

Dr Celeste inserted his hands into heavy rubber gloves integrated into the glass cabinet. Carefully, he placed the frame containing her frozen tears into a container that released wisps of liquid nitrogen.

"Follow me," he said.

In another room of gleaming white, Dr Celeste transferred the frozen tears into the belly of a broad, metallic cylinder. He sat at a laptop in front of the cylinder and keyed in commands. Bolts clanged into place and the cylinder sang with a low hum.

"What now?" asked Isabel.

"In layman's terms, I'm using a quantum processor to map sub-atomic particle activity within the tear. The code I have written will reconstruct the activity as images; it will translate pure physics into a visual format we can process."

"*Layman's terms*," said Isabel, with a smile. "You must know some *very* clever laymen."

"Well, I..." Dr Celeste doesn't finish the sentence.

Isabel smiled again. "Nevermind, what images have you found in the other tears you have tested?"

"Just hints."

"Hints of what?"

"Unhappiness."

"But surely..."

"Wait," said Dr Celeste, holding up a hand. The computer had shed all text and was filling with grey lines.

The process was slow, and at first Isabel thought the lines were nothing but interference, digital static. But then she saw her mother's eyes revealed, line by line. Her long nose. The image was grainy, like a newspaper photograph repeatedly photocopied. It moved: *her mother tossing her head from side to side on her pillow; her lips gummed closed; eyes scrambling for purchase on the world; she mouthed Isabel's name.*

"How can this be?"

Dr Celeste stroked a finger up Isabel's cheek and collected a tear on the tip of his finger. For a second, he held it to his eye and then rubbed it between finger and thumb.

"The previous images were nowhere near as distinct as this," he said.

Isabel wiped tears from her eyes and looked at them smeared across her palms. Her mother's face was now still and frozen on the screen. "This is the most amazing thing I have ever seen. You must show it to the world."

"It isn't for the world. It's for me. This is a personal project," said Dr Celeste. He stabbed a key and Isabel's mother disappeared. "Don't worry, I have a back-up."

Isabel felt anger at Dr Celeste casually cancelling her link to the past. She took a breath; reigned in her emotions. He was a scientist. This was research. "What do you mean, a personal project?"

Dr Celeste hesitated, as if unsure whether to reveal anything further to her. He closed his eyes and tapped his chest above his heart. "I'm trying to find out what is missing from myself. What is missing in here? I experience emotions at a such a low level. I'm what people call a *cold fish* or a *human computer*. I always have been. I need to understand why. To do so, I need a template, a baseline, to establish the shape of others' emotions. Thanks to you, I have taken a huge step forward in that understanding."

Gratitude and desire overwhelmed Isabel. What an effort it must have been for him to reveal this to a stranger. To a woman. This was a cry to her. A challenge.

"But now I face a virtually insurmountable problem in my research," said Dr Celeste.

"Surely no problem is insurmountable."

He released a small laugh, an anguished sound like a call from a caged laboratory animal. "I have never cried."

Isabel cocked her head. "Never?"

"Never." Dr Celeste held up his hands. "And I must cry naturally. An artificially extracted tear is of no use to me."

"Then I will help you cry," said Isabel.

"And how do you propose to do that?"

"I'm an actress. It is one of my areas of expertise."

Dr Celeste paused. "Ms Lacombe, I accept your offer."

"You'd have to submit yourself totally to me."

"I still accept."

"And you must promise to call me Isabel."

Dr Celeste's acceptance thrilled Isabel. Now they were operating in her area of expertise and she could actively influence their relationship.

They retired to Dr Celeste's living quarters, which were only marginally less spartan and cold than the laboratory. Isabel began to question him. She probed into his past, seeking phobias and repression and guilt. As an infant, he had rarely seen his politician father, who was forever on the campaign trail. His mother fluttered around the bright lights of society, appalled by the mundanity of child rearing. He had no siblings. He set himself rituals of learning from a very early age, shunning friendship when it interfered with his studies. The rituals became ingrained through school and university and on into adult life.

Isabel tried to jab at his absence of love and companionship, to raise the ghost of emotion, but Dr Celeste's answers were cool and factual. Isabel groped around in his private life, trying to find evidence of broken hearts or betrayal, of frustration, desire or perversion – there was nothing.

She halted her questioning and drank a glass of wine that Dr Celeste offered her. Her frustration at her inability to reach him was making *her* emotional. She savoured the wine and composed herself. She would have to try an alternative approach.

Isabel's palm slapped against his cheek, turning his face and leaving a red welt.

"Bastard," she said. For a second she saw the flicker of *something* in his eyes. She slapped him again, this time on the other cheek. "Stop teasing me. Tell me the truth. Let it go."

"What do I *have* to let go of?" said Dr Celeste, rubbing his cheeks.

"Your facade."

"My facade?"

"Tell me why you asked me to come, Pascal."

"To be part of my research."

"Really?" Isabel slapped him again. "Tell me the truth."

"That is the truth."

Isabel stood and approached Dr Celeste. The confusion on his face excited her; cracks in his armour. She lifted her skirt and straddled his knees, draped her arms around his neck and kissed him. His lips were cold and unresponsive. She pressed herself hard against him, moving her groin against his legs, sliding her tongue into his mouth. He responded by putting his tongue in her mouth and swivelling it around like a dentist's mirror searching for cavities.

She pulled away from him and slapped him again. She was breathing heavily and close to tears. This was like dashing herself against a block of ice. She had ransacked his past and he hadn't blinked an eye. She had offered herself to him and he had shown not the slightest response. She raised her arms and sighed in temporary defeat.

"Let me make you another drink," said Dr Celeste.

Isabel nodded and slumped back into her chair. Dr Celeste handed her the drink and sat opposite her again.

She gulped down the wine. Her frustration made it taste slightly bitter, but it soothed her nerves. She sighed and put her head in her hands.

Then she heard Dr Celeste emit a strangled sound. When she looked up, she saw a single tear sliding down his cheek. He was holding his head back, trying to preserve the precious fluid.

"Quickly, the glass slide," he said.

With shaking hands, Isabel collected his tear.

"Thank you," he said.

With infinite care, he carried the precious tear to the freezing room and then onto the radiation cylinder. Throughout, Dr Celeste was silent with concentration.

Isabel was feeling lightheaded. Too much wine and the intense emotional mining she had carried out on Dr Celeste's history. She squinted at the screen, desperate to see what image or memory had finally moved Dr Celeste to tears.

The cylinder ceased humming and the computer terminal replaced strings of data with an empty screen. Isabel could feel Dr Celeste's shoulder rubbing against hers. Her eyes were tired and so she leant against him. He no longer felt cold and distant. She had been the one to help him overcome his insurmountable problem.

Grey lines scrawled across the screen from top to bottom. The picture was not clear. Feet? A bed? No, a hospital trolley. A body on a hospital trolley. What memory could this be? Isabel turned to look at Dr Celeste's face, but as she did so she nearly lost balance and toppled from her chair. Dr Celeste put an arm around her to keep her in place. She smiled. His hands were warm. Her head lolled back to centre so she could see the screen.

The grainy image had jerked into life. Somebody was

wheeling a stretcher down a corridor. She recognised it. It was the corridor that ran along outside the room they were in. She tried to face Dr Celeste, but her neck muscles were slack and uncooperative.

What was happening to her? She tried to speak, but her lips remained closed. Although she could see the reflection of Dr Celeste's arm around her shoulders in the screen, she couldn't feel it. Her body was numb. She remembered the bitter taste of the wine.

On the screen, the stretcher pushed through a set of double doors and into a room. Across the room. A hand opened a large white door. Wisps of vapour curled away from the door frame. The stretcher wheeled inside. On the shelves of the room were the frozen bodies of eight women. Hands lifted the woman on the stretcher onto a shelf to make nine.

A view of the bright ceiling lights replaced the image on the screen as Dr Celeste lifted Isabel into his arms and placed her onto the stretcher. His face came into view as he secured straps across her chest. There was a second tear sliding down his cheek.

"I'm sorry," he said. "But nobody must know. This is for me."

STILL LIVES IN MOTION

The girl with the puffer jacket and leopard-skin mobile phone cover – the laughing girl – she will be the first to die, he thinks. *Bang*! Straight in the face. Then her coven of mates. Move on. Pump it. Aim. The lads mock-fighting, flipping the brims of each other's baseball caps, trying to spin them over the bannister to the lower level of the mall, into the seething sea of over-stressed Christmas shoppers hauling brats, bodies glowing red and sickly blue from the blinking lights of the twenty-feet-high Nordic spruce donated by a Scandinavian twin town.

Bang. Bang. Bang.

Blood on the concourse.

People screaming and slipping. The old man with the eyes that say: *waster* –*bang*, bye bye. The mothers and fathers that steer their precious, precocious bundles of snot well clear of him: *bang, bang*. The girls with their jiggling tits and eyes for others. The boys drunk with attitude. All of them. *Bang, bang, bang*! He will kill all of them.

Bang.

He slams the toilet door too hard.

Bang.

The long bag slung over and biting into his shoulder hits the side of the cubicle – metal on laminated wood. The buzz of the zip and then he has cold metal in his hands. Hot sweat on a clammy brow. He can hear their noise even in the cubicle. They yap and stammer and holler. They deserve what's coming to them. For what they have done to him. For what they would have continued to do to him. For keeping him locked in this loveless vacuum. Time to puncture the container.

He rests his head against the cubicle wall, breathes deeply, knowing the last hurdle of doubt has long been vaulted. He's sliding back the bolt, opening the door and walking. He glimpses himself in the mirror - ginger ponytail tied back, chickenpox scars clustered on his cheeks. His gaze is distant, seeing the truth, the future, seeing what needs to be done.

Through the toilet entrance. Now there is just a corridor and another door at the end separating him from his destiny. From release. I have nothing, he thinks. I am empty. His soles slap linoleum purposefully. He raises the shotgun, adjusting his stance. He can hear their great babble behind the door. That great unfocused, materialistic chant. A choir sings Silent Night. He opens the door...

...AND THE WORLD IS SILENT.

The mall is empty.

He stands motionless. An animal expecting a trap, ready to bolt for cover when the pretence ends. His pulse roars in his ears and his heart punches his ribs. Slowly, he calms himself and realises that the world is not silent. He can hear a radio playing in a shop to his left. Elsewhere there are the sounds of automated advertising. All the lighting is on and it hums its purposeful note. Escalators grind round and round. The world continues but without its creators. The people are gone. He is alone in the mall.

It cannot be. He breaks from statue stillness and weaves through the cafeteria tables, which moments before had hosted his tormentors, and peers over the balcony. The Christmas tree lights bathe the dirty floor red and blue, red and blue. No crowds. No people.

He calls out, "Hello?"

No reply except an automated Santa ho-ho-ho-ing his way through a sales pitch. Sam turns and squeezes the trigger, blowing Santa to melted red shards. Smoke curls up and out of the remaining stumps of his legs. There is no response to the blast of the shotgun. No screams or sirens or shouts of horror and indignation.

He's laughing now as he runs through deserted corridors, caught between delirium and fear. The people have all disappeared. Then, a hitch in his sudden elation: *what if they haven't gone? Maybe there was a fire alarm and I didn't hear it. What if they're all waiting for me outside?*

Down the escalator, following exit signs, breath raw in his lungs, a hundred yards along a walkway and the automatic doors swish open onto the main street. It's snowing. It's empty. The silence is overpowering. He fills the silence with laughter and gunshots for as long as he has breath and ammunition, then he collapses and lies back, listening to the silence and staring up into the patterns of falling snow thinking: *this new world is mine and I shall cherish it.*

IT IS New Year before Sam is prepared to accept that he is now alone in the world. He has travelled back to his flat – driving wildly along snowy streets in a BMW he *borrowed* from a deserted garage – and found it as he left it, but devoid of neighbours. Electricity still flows through cables and gas through pipes, but the TV shows nothing but a hissing screen, the radio plays nothing but static. He drives out to a power station – in a four-wheel-drive Suzuki that he drove out through the plate-glass window of a display room – and although the turbines whirr with life, there are no employees pressing buttons or grimacing over flickering dials. It works for him alone. Maybe it's magic. Maybe it's the power of thought. *Maybe I've removed myself to somewhere to just to the side of everybody else. A place just for me.* Until New Year, he wakes every day expecting to find the beautiful dream ended and his persecutors returned. But he remains alone. Beautifully isolated. When New Year arrives, he wakes without fear. He knows this is his world.

On Twelfth Night he takes down all the Christmas decorations in the shopping centre. He takes weeks to remove all the baubles and tinsel but he isn't worried about bad luck; this is a new world and there has to be leeway given while he becomes its master.

He decides to live in the shopping centre. This is where it started. The trigger for his emancipation. He sets up home in the furniture section of a well-known department store. He doesn't use its name – that was theirs, now it is his. He just calls it number fifty-six.

Number fifty-six has everything that he needs. Furniture, lighting, even a working demonstration cooker in the appliances section. Its food hall is stuffed with enough tins and microwave meals to last for years. Next door is a freezer shop.

His days are never empty. Across from number fifty-six is a bookshop and he sets himself the task of reading every book. He picks a unique spot to read every day. When spring arrives unrolling warmer, brighter skies, he favours a perch on the roof, so he can survey his city and listen to bird song

Summer arrives. He tires of his book-reading project and moves on. He has DVDs aplenty and the town's well-stocked adult shops offer all the sexual solace he needs. He devises other distractions. Pretending to work a day at the office. Forcing himself to rise at eight and then drive to an office and tap away at a nonsense spreadsheet for four hours, eating a packed lunch in the park, a few more hours casually tapping away at his spreadsheet and then drinks in a local pub followed by a microwave curry in a Balti house. He forces himself to throw up on the steps of the police station. All is well with the world, he thinks the following day, as he wakes with a hangover and rolls over waiting for recuperative sleep to claim him again.

Winter returns and he takes up a new project in the city's cinemas. By a frustrating process of trial and error, he teaches himself how to play films. In the city's arthouse cinema he sits alone, watching Charlton Heston sitting alone, watching a film of Woodstock in *The Omega Man*. *Tough luck on the zombie/vampire front, Chuck. Nobody here but me and the birds.*

Christmas comes again. He puts up the shopping centre's decorations a month ahead of time. They did it for commerce. He does it because he takes that long. The following year he repeats his projects. Adds a few new ones. Two years becomes three and then seems to skip to five.

It is January of the fifth year when the torpor begins to afflict him. All his projects are on hold. The bookshop houses too many texts he does not enjoy or understand and he has already reread his favourites rather than risk disappointment. He knows every scene in every porn film available to him. He has rebuilt his department-store apartment a hundred times. Worn every set of clothes – male and female – on offer and even spent weeks naked. He has spent his energy on running wild and now he cannot recharge himself because he has nothing to push against. Nobody to oppose him and provide the fire of his certainties. In his own way he is lonely, missing those he despised so heartily. The silence is sapping his energy. He has begun to dream of his last moments in the old world. A dream burning with the guilt of the atrocities he might have committed. He keeps waking in the night. When he stares at himself in the mirror, his eyes are red and tired. His body creaks.

Sleet and wind fill January days. He can do nothing but shelter inside the shopping centre, eyes closed as he sits in the concourse restaurant where it all began, listening to loud music playing over the tannoy. He knows the music so well it soothes him. He sings along under his breath. But today something is wrong with it. It's changing. New words. A voice calling out from the heart of the song. A voice. Then his blood becomes ice. He walks to the railing and looks down to the ground floor.

She is standing bundled in a heavy coat. A woolly hat pulled down over her ears. Her face, in particular her nose, red from the cold. She collapses to the floor and cries, pointing up and him, laughter and tears causing snot to dribble from that red nose.

"You're real," she says and sobs helplessly.

THE FIRST COUPLE of weeks are the worst for him. Another person. He suspects that his idyll is about to be taken away from him, that her arrival heralds the return of the persecuting masses, pressing back into his shopping centre, filling it like poison gas. He spends a lot of time on the roof, scanning the surrounding area with high-powered binoculars, straining his ears for the telltale sound of engines, helicopters, voices. He hears and sees nothing. His panic recedes.

She tells him that her name is Jennifer. He tells her his name. She had been living in the north of the country when everybody disappeared, and it had happened on the same day as his deliverance. She is more talkative than he is, but what she says interests and even thrills him. It is not the senseless patter of those others that he so despised. She is like him. One of the first things she says is:

"I'm not sad that they're all gone."

She did not have a happy life and she did not feel part of the old world. She had desperately wanted to be away from it, although she did not know how this could be achieved.

"They made me feel worthless," she says.

He smiles at this. Her words make him feel warm inside.

"They were all bastards," he says, and they both laugh.

He shows her his world.

The more they talk, the more they find they have in common. Both of them were content to live alone in their new world for the first few years, doing as they pleased, finally feeling at peace with themselves, but in the last year a sense of listlessness has settled upon them. That is why Jennifer has moved from city to city, working her way south, seeking others who might have escaped to her brave new world.

Summer comes and they sit on the shopping-centre roof, reading books and listening to the birds. A question, heavy and as uncomfortable as a rock in his head. He knows it's linked to a ghost of guilt; his own actions just before the old world vanished. Finally, he asks her the question.

"What were you doing... just before it happened?"

She pretends not to hear him, squinting hard at her book. He asks her again and he can see something desperate in her eyes. Black emotions darting like fish, magnified by sudden, swelling tears. She shakes her head. Sunlit tears on her cheeks. She stands and runs away.

It is a week before she returns and the pain caused by her absence scares him. He could rejoice in the world's annihilation, but a week without Jennifer tears at his insides. How can this be?

When she returns, she apologises. "It's too painful," she says. "Promise me you won't ask me about that again."

Her apology is like a kiss on his soul. Nobody ever apologised to him before. Not with meaning. Not with tenderness in their voice. He promises. They embrace. A blissful embrace which extends through the night as the only two people in the world press together as one.

AS THE YEARS PASS, they transform their shopping centre into a palace. It is their shared project. The king and queen of the world deserve a residence worthy of their station, and they scour the city and the surrounding area to make it so. Their bedroom is an entire floor of the department store with a maze of brocade curtains leading to the

four-poster bed at the centre. Their bath is a small swimming pool that once served the luxury apartments atop the
centre. They tile it with mirrors and light it with a thousand
candles, making the water amber. Their dining room is the
ground floor of the centre and, to amuse themselves, they
sometimes arrange table after table in a long line, him sitting
at one end, her at the other, separated by fifty feet of
candlelit table, chatting to each other on walkie-talkies. One
perfect night, they eat on a rooftop table, a beaming full
moon as witness to their contentment, and she tells him she
loves him. After that, his dreams turn dark.

For years he struggles to stifle the dark dreams, but he is
in their grip. How could he not be? The dreams are a ghost
of the other world, as if his sleeping mind is trying to
continue the old life he left behind – the dream equivalent
of a phantom limb. In his dreams, when he opens the door
from the toilets, the shopping centre is not deserted, it is as
crowded and as noisy and full of seething selfishness as
before. Heads turn towards him. The young man with the
shotgun. He feels steel and wood in his hands. They speak
to him. The language of recoil and reload, air-tearing noise
and body-shredding shrapnel. He lays waste to the restaurant, drowning in fear and blood and the knowledge that he
has sealed his world of misery. There is no release in that
world.

Wakefulness is his only release.

And he knows that Jennifer has dark dreams too. Sometimes, when he forces himself to stay awake, he sees her
wrestle with her night demons, unintelligible words
bubbling from her lips, fear creasing her face. Sometimes
there are tears. He does not ask her about the dream,
because he knows instinctively he'll be asking her about the
moment. He has promised her he would not ask, but the

desire to know, the fact that what happened to her might help him cope with his own demons, is a painful pressure inside him. Maybe she is ready to talk now? Can he take the risk?

They struggle on, pretending to be content, but when they look into each other's eyes, they can see the truth. Their dreams of the old world are eating them from the inside, devouring them so they will soon not exist in this world. There is a desperate pleading in her eyes. She knows he will ask her about her dreams.

"It might help us both," he says.

"You promised," she says.

He grips her arms tight and shakes her. His fear of losing this world, of losing her, makes him shout. "This is our only chance."

She closes her eyes and shakes her head. Through her sobs, she tells him of how she rose from the bath of warm water – the tap still running, the blade of the cutthroat razor still pressed against her artery, needing only a movement of millimetres to begin the end – as the world went silent around her. It was the unearthly quality of the silence that made her draw back from the point of desperation.

"I had nothing, but it would have been a mortal sin," she said. "The silence offered me hope."

"It was the same for me," he says, but she is walking away from him, crying.

"You promised," she says.

"I had to ask you for us. It was the only way."

She turns and looks at him. "You made me go back," she says, and then she leaves.

THIS TIME she does not return after a week, or two, or a month. He searches for her across the city and beyond, but there is no hint of her. He is alone in their palace. Alone in their world. Misery. As miserable as he was in the last moments in the old world. His dreams seize upon his misery as a sign to redouble their assault upon him, dragging him through a painful ghost life, where he is pilloried as a virulent snatcher of lives by a world he hates and hates him in equal measures.

She has left him like all the others, and now the dreams feed on him. He realises that he must exorcise them or this world will crumble. His solution is desperate, but he can think of no alternative. He will show the dream he is not afraid of it.

The shopping centre's restaurant has long been dismantled – it did not fit in with their designs for the palace – but he has all the tables and fittings stored, and now he rebuilds it from memory. Next he positions shop mannequins, dressed as accurately as he can recall, at the tables, positioning them so they appear to be eating or drinking, chatting. He finds a dusty old leopard-skin mobile phone and tapes it to the hand of one of the shop dummies. As he looks at his handiwork, déjà vu makes him feel nauseous.

Inside the toilet, he slots shells into the shotgun. No hesitation. He will blast the dreams away. He strides down the corridor, bursts through the door and starts firing at the mannequins. Deafening noise, plastic limbs and heads flying, clothes on fire, windows shattering. He yells above it all. Firing in an arc. One of the dummies stands waving its arms at him and still yelling, he blasts it in the stomach. It screams and stumbles backwards. *She* screams and stumbles backwards. Collapses onto her side, blood spreading across linoleum.

Deafening noise receding.

He sobs as he leans over Jennifer. Blood runs from her mouth. He pulls her towards him. He still has the shotgun in one hand. He rocks her and says repeatedly that he is sorry.

She smiles briefly and whispers, "I came back to forgive you." Then she is gone. He fills the silence with a wail of loss. Nausea rises in him and he releases her, stumbles away, bouncing between the tables, back into the bathroom, and vomits violently. He leans against the cold porcelain, crying. *I cannot leave her out there like that*, he thinks. He pulls himself to his feet on jelly legs, the shotgun fused to his hand like an extension of his murderous limb. Down the corridor, dreading the sight of her body, the devastation he has wrought.

THE WALL of noise smacks into him like heat as he opens the door. The restaurant is full of people. The same people. Conversations clatter back and forth for a few moments and then all eyes turn towards him. Screams and gasps as they see the shotgun in his hand and the desolation on his face. The scraping of chairs as people flee.

They should not have worried. He does not even see them. He has caught his reflection in a shop window and he sees all the years he accrued in the other world, the world where he was a king and had a queen, have sloughed away. He is a young man again. But he is changed: he is only young on the outside; on the inside he has lived a life, he has loved and lost. He is no longer empty.

Policemen edge towards him, talking calmly, telling him to put down the shotgun. He does as they tell him and he feels arms grasp him violently, dragging him to the floor, pinning his arms behind his back. Handcuffs rasp shut. They haul him to his feet.

I have loved and lost, he thinks. *I know how it feels to live. I need not concern myself with these people. I can find her here. She isn't dead, not here, not in this world.* He doesn't know how he is so sure of this, he just feels it as a burning certainty. He smiles as they lead him away, picturing Jennifer closing the razor and smiling as she says his name.

THE GALILEAN MANOEUVRE

The first time I saw her, she was lost in the red mist of an argument. Her energy fizzed against a backdrop of the drugged and drunk. A bouncer dwarfed her, threatening to throw her out of the club. The throb of techno beats drowned out their dialogue. Pulsing lights created cubist expressions. She poked him in the chest and he pointed towards the exit. Slowly, she backed away from him. Three beer bottles appeared in her hands and she began juggling; catching each by its neck and sending it through multiple spins, before catching it with the opposite hand and launching it into a reverse arc.

Her movements transfixed the bouncer. A crowd gathered around them. The pace of the surrounding music increased as a strobe filled the room with a manic flicker. The bottles moved like frames in a zoetrope. Suddenly, one bottle disappeared. The bouncer searched the air for it. Now she was juggling two bottles with her left hand. The third bottle was in her right hand and I watched it arc upwards and smash into the bouncer's chin. He collapsed, clutching his bloody jaw. The girl smiled down at him and spat. She had a beauty spot of blood on her cheek. She disappeared into the crowd.

I caught up with her in the street outside the club.

"That was a cool trick," I said.

"It wasn't a *trick*. I was juggling," she said.

"It was great juggling."

"It was slack."

"My father was a professional juggler, I should know." An effortless lie; a professional reaction.

She stopped and turned to look up at me. Her face was handsome rather than pretty and she radiated energy, a fierce heat that made mere surface attraction irrelevant. I wanted to use her to warm the cold, dark place inside me, even if it was for just a night.

"Are you giving me a line?"

"Watch." I removed my shoes, ignoring the wet pavement, and juggled. "Da-da"

She unlaced one of her clumpy trainers and threw it at me. I worked it into the circling loop of shoes. Her other trainer sailed through the air to my left and I shifted my balance, my socks slapping like flippers, and the four shoes passed smoothly before my eyes. She was watching with the faintest of smiles, curling her toes against the wet concrete.

"So you followed in your father's footsteps," she said.

"Oh no – I'm a journalist."

"Never mind." She scratched her chin. "Want to come home with me?"

I lost control of the shoes, and they bounced around me. "What's your name?"

"Hero."

"Yes I would, Hero."

MRS BALVENIE LET several hacking sobs escape her chest, then breathed deeply into her handkerchief. As she leant forward to blow her nose, I noticed how greasy and unkempt her hair had become over the past week. Although I could empathise with her disintegration, I could not afford to spare her.

"I've made my decision. I don't want to give you any more details. I can't do it to them." She pointed at a pair of portraits. Her children. *Their* children. "It finishes now."

I unleashed an internal wail while trying unsuccessfully to maintain a full-beam expression of concern and understanding. I thought I'd snared a ravening beast, a story with teeth enough to devour a celebrity, but it was mutating into a gummy no-hoper before my eyes. I'd staked my resurrection on this, planning to ride it triumphantly into the newsroom, while my humble colleagues lined my path with the bloody garments of former victims.

"Jane." I had to go personal, root for emotions. "That shit of a husband has treated you disgracefully. This is your opportunity – your only opportunity – for *revenge.*"

"I'm sick of revenge. It's like heroin. You never get enough until it's destroyed you. I don't want anymore."

"My wife left me for another man." This was less a lie than a heresy, but the greater the weight to move, the longer the lever required. "I understand what you are going through."

"Then you know what it feels like to have love and hate twist around your heart and squeeze until there is nothing left. Except emptiness. I want something other than revenge to fill the vacuum."

She scored with that one. I hesitated. "Mrs Balvenie—"

"I want you to go now. I have no more to say."

Outside her house I called my editor, ready to twist lies

into pretty shapes, then thought better of it. I dialled off; phoned Hero instead. She wasn't home.

I'D BEEN SEEING Hero for the last month – whenever she could fit me in between practising and performing her juggling routine – and she remained a frustrating paradox. She could be so arrogant, distant and downright disturbing that she had me humming at the edge of violence. But she balanced this with intoxicating moods of playfulness and physical intensity; moments when the heat of her desire surged through me, warming the hollow space inside my shell.

She soon discovered that my juggling abilities did not extend beyond my initial display, and I had no ambition to develop them. She shifted her attention to my father, continually interrogating me about his career and experiences. This became so intense, and I became so tired of keeping track of all my lies, I told her he'd died recently and that talking about him made me sad. Eventually, she stopped asking questions.

She was only twenty-one years of age, a drama student – although nothing except juggling seemed to interest her – and she shared a house with a group of other would-be thespians. I'd stayed over at their house frequently and was usually treated with the disdain that those in their early twenties reserve for those in their thirties.

My chief tormentor was Milt. He claimed to be Hero's best friend, but I rarely saw them do anything other than argue. He had curly hair that had grown unruly and covered his eyes. He was always sucking on a joint and expounding on one of his theories.

The only teacher worth learning from, he would say, is one that has himself been taught by a master. All crafts and arts have their originating master, and this master once poured his knowledge into one pupil, who then passed it on to his protégé in the next generation. Each generation refines the knowledge, expands it, searches for the boundaries and then crosses them.

But teachers have more than one pupil, I'd argue, without interest, as I waited for Hero to change or shower or find a more congenial mood.

True masters have only one pupil, Milt would say. The others just pass on watered-down truths and their teaching diminishes into banality. Only those carrying the core knowledge are driven to seek the forbidden boundaries of their disciplines; mad, beautiful, Icarus-angels embracing the sun.

Mad, beautiful, Icarus-angels embracing the sun. And students wonder why people think they're wankers.

Milt would never be my friend. And I didn't believe a word he inflicted on me.

TAYLOR HAD a face like a crushed beer can, an implosion of wrinkles and folds of skin. He finished his Scotch and sipped his pint. The jabber of drunk journalists was deafening. I was heavy-headed and slow, the room slowly tilting on its axis whenever I lifted my pint. I felt I might fall from my seat and tumble towards the exit and out into the street. That wouldn't have been pleasant, because God had been on a bender too and he was taking a raging horse piss onto our stinking city.

"They're after me," I said.

"They're always after someone," said Taylor. "If you run with the hounds, make sure you don't so much as nick yourself shaving. It's all they need. Did they find out about Ellie?"

I nodded. Somebody bumped into me as I raised my pint and beer slopped down my sleeve, dribbling down my forearm, taking a sharp left at my elbow and chilling my armpit.

Taylor downed half his pint. He was an old hand, a legend on the paper. The more he filled the space inside him with booze, the more real he became. "If they smell spilt blood, there is only one thing you can do."

"What?"

"Get out your knife and spill somebody else's blood."

MILT TOLD me Hero was downstairs and, with a dismissive look at my tuxedo, disappeared into another room. Hero had built herself a gym in the cellar so she could keep her body toned for her juggling routines.

I turned off the music as I entered. She was lying on a low bench, curling dumbbells across her chest.

"You were supposed to meet me three hours ago. I had tickets for a premiere, remember? The premiere you wanted to go to. I had to grovel for these tickets."

Hero sat up on the bench. Her grey crop top and cycle shorts were soaked with sweat. She was panting. "I forgot," she said.

"That's it? I forgot? No apology. No grovelling of your own. Just: I forgot."

"I just found out that one of Europe's greatest underground jugglers has a gig tomorrow night. I have to be ready," she said.

Underground juggler. Spare me. "I suppose he's one of Milt's master jugglers?"

"As a matter of fact, he is."

"Maybe you can become his protégé," I snorted.

"Maybe," she said.

I turned away and stalked towards the door, trying to hurl a final, concussive insult in her direction, but I only squeezed out a snarl. As I opened the door, her feet padded on the floor and suddenly her legs were around my waist. I turned in her grip. She had fixed a pull-up bar just above the door, and she was dangling from it. She pulled herself up so that her damp breasts pressed into my face. Her musky sweat made me breathless.

"I'll make it up to you," she whispered.

I ripped off her shorts and entered her as she dangled from the bar, cords and knots of muscle straining her skin. Then she told me to tie her to the exercise bench. There were burn marks on her wrist when I'd finished. I lay curled over her back, panting.

"I went to see your wife today," she said.

The world stopped. The cold place inside of me throbbed painfully. "You what?"

"Your wife. I went to see her."

"I... you..." Nothing. No more words.

"She still limps from the time you threw her down the stairs," said Hero.

I unwound myself from Hero and pulled on my crumpled clothes. "I never hit her," I said, searching myself for anger or self-hate, but finding only ice and lies.

"Why did you do it?"

"I didn't do anything."

"Liar."

"You know nothing about me."

Hero laughed. "Oh yes I do. I can feel the weight of you."

I COULD BARELY CONTROL the poisonous adrenalin pulsing through me as I offered praise to the merciful god of persistence. An unlikely interview had led to a cataclysmic revelation. I was ready to leap onto the back of my beastly story, grab its reins and rend and trample anyone who dared so much as to question my competence.

Reluctantly, Mrs Balvenie ushered me in. "Who was it?" she asked.

"Your niece." *Whoosh!* Two words as sharp as swords – *off with the fucker's head.* The poison pumped through my body, filling my mouth, glowing in my eyes. "He had sex with your fifteen-year-old niece."

But Mrs Balvenie held my gaze, despite her tears, despite the humiliation and pain. "He's dead to me now. I still have nothing to say."

My mouth opened to beg and cajole, but it was full of poison and it made me dumb. I rushed from her house and the poison gushed from my throat.

HERO HELD me in her arms and rocked me back and forwards as we lay on my bed. The chaos of my life lay scattered around us in piles of unwashed clothes, ripped files, empty bottles and moldy plates. Coffee-cup stains formed chains on my bedside table. How long had I been living like this? Ice had eaten away my insides and I felt brittle enough to shatter if she squeezed too hard.

I hadn't expected her to come, but I had nobody else to call. She had arrived at my house within twenty minutes. A burning, capricious angel to warm this husk of a man.

"Come with me this evening," she said.

How could I refuse?

THE VENUE WAS a renovated warehouse beside the river. The walls had been decorated with huge, aggressive canvases of blurred and straining anatomy; student love letters to Francis Bacon. Sharp steel sculptures stood sentinel in the bar. A death-slow bassline vibrated through me and I tried to fill myself with alcohol. I needed ballast.

I stayed close to the glow of Hero. She wandered through the crowd, hugging and kissing and joking with the freaks milling around us. Now and then she should smile at me or kiss me feverishly, biting my lip. Most of the time she ignored me and I just followed her light, while drinking and drinking. Milt was there. He blew me a kiss across the room and drew a finger across his throat. I tried to avoid his eyes after that.

A stage had been set up in the main room, with tables and chairs arrayed in front of it, and we sat down with some of Hero's friends. Lights pulsed continually and my eyes ached. I had to squint to see. I tipped more alcohol into my body but I might as well have been trying to fill the Grand Canyon. My vision had blurred. Nobody was paying any attention to me, so I rested my head against the table for a time. When I raised it again, the show had begun. A huge screen had been suspended above the stage, replaying the action with a delay of several seconds.

"Where's the *master*?" I slurred to Hero, but she continued to ignore me. People sharing our table turned to look at us and I sneered in reply and then laughed to myself.

A series of juggling acts *graced* the stage; jugglers with fire, jugglers with animals, jugglers with shit. The lights and the alcohol and the whole pathetic spectacle were just too much. I put my head on my arms and closed my eyes again.

When I opened them next, I thought I had gone blind – every light in the room had been extinguished. A spotlight lanced through the blackness and an old man walked to centre stage. His weathered face filled the screen, and even the dismal video resolution could not diminish the energy in his eyes.

I could not understand him when he spoke. People around me were nodding in agreement and occasionally laughing, or bursting into applause, but as hard as I tried I couldn't understand the garbled nonsense.

Was I that drunk?

"I'm not that drunk," I said to Hero.

No reply.

The old man juggled. I squinted at the screen as rubber balls lined with tiny needles bit into his palms and fingers, flecking his face with blood as they arced past his eyes. Then there were small animals, flayed and pink, that squealed each time they slapped against his salt-covered hands. Finally, there was fire – raw, unhoused fire – tossed from hand to hand, until the room smelt of burnt flesh.

The audience was applauding. Hero was bouncing on her seat like a child watching a clown for the very first time. Even I knew this was wrong. I had to leave. When I tried to stand, powerful hands pushed me back into my seat.

The old man was speaking again, standing at the front of the stage, looking into the crowd. A spotlight engulfed our table, blinding me. Applause rang out and people banged their hands rhythmically against the tables. I was being led to the stage.

The old man's face was close to mine. "You dared, but you failed," he whispered.

I didn't know what he meant, but it could have been a reference to any of a dozen major catastrophes in my life. But the insouciance with which he spoke lit a spark of anger in my icy soul. Anger leant me strength and I lunged towards him. "I haven't failed. I —"

The anger was spent too quickly and I was easily manhandled onto a table. There were people on the stage. They removed my shirt and stuck tape across my mouth. Broad plastic straps secured me to the wood. Hero appeared above me and kissed my tape-covered lips. She had a scalpel in her hand.

"It took me a while to find the weight of you," she said.

The old man stood at her side. I writhed and bucked against the straps, screaming silently as he nodded to her.

I did not feel the incision. Maybe my hollow and icy chest had just caved in on itself. Applause lapped around me as Hero held a glistening organ aloft. Maybe I had been dead for a long time and not known it. She placed my heart on the table and lifted a saw. Its teeth bit into my neck, ripping my Adam's apple and juddering against my spine. It was just a dull, mechanical sensation. There wasn't any pain. Maybe the ice had killed all my nerves.

Life on ice. Ha ha!

I saw the room whirl around me as Hero juggled with my heart and head. Lights flashing and shifting. A blur of ever-changing faces, alight with smiles of awe, flesh slapping together in appreciation. More lights. A constellation. Hero's body aglow, pulsing with power. The speed increasing. The rhythmic banging of hands on tables. Noise and colour bleeding into one long, bright blur.

I closed my eyes.

A NEW DAWN.

Grey morning light was worming its way through a partially blacked out skylight. The smell of spilt beer and sweat. I was naked. I expected to see a livid and puckered scar across my chest. It was unmarked. My throat was aflame. Pain brought forth tears when I coughed. I found a piece of broken mirror and saw that my neck was similarly unmarked.

I remembered the lights, the scalpel and the saw. Hero juggling.

What had she done to me? I had no tools to analyse or rationalise what had happened. Maybe I shouldn't try. Maybe I'd lose this strange but comforting sense of calm if I did.

She'd changed me.

I laughed out loud and then winced as pain branched out through my nerves. I no longer felt like an icy husk; there was movement inside; the flickering flame of mystery and madness.

They'd abused me but left me with some new life.

I stood on the stage and gathered two beer bottles. I mimed the roars and applause of a crowd as I juggled. When I fumbled the bottles, they smashed, shards skittering across the stage, but I picked up two more and started again.

DARWIN'S BOY

Jerome hauls his body into the lowest branches of the Tree. Feels them sway and bend beneath his weight. Slowly, his trembling palms spread against the trunk, he stands. He presses his cheek against ridged bark, relishing its rough solidity. He hates heights. Especially heights that sway in the wind. But this is his sanctuary. Where else could he hide from the Horde?

Reaching into the dense cluster of branches above, he finds a sturdy handhold and scrambles up through a ceiling of sappy leaves to a height where he is hidden from the ground.

He lowers himself into a sitting position on a branch. He breathes deeply, but as quietly as possible, to catch his breath. Sweat soaks his T-shirt. It sticks to his back and front. Flies and pollen-drunk bees buzz into his personal space, then dexterously avoid the sweep of his hand. It's stiflingly hot, again. The air itself seems to buzz and throb, as if this endless heatwave has angered every atom in existence. The Town is miles away, but he can hear sirens whining. Police? Ambulances? Probably both. Violence and sickness are increasingly common. There are always sirens these days.

Another sound. Voices approaching.

Jerome shifts his position. Peers down between his feet. His movements snap free a leaf. It propellers towards the ground.

Roddy and three of the Horde strut into view. *Walk on by, walk on by, please, please, walk on by.* Jerome mouths the prayer. But they don't.

"Here," says Roddy, leaning against the base of the tree.

An adolescent with a sunburned face speckled with erupting acne produces a spliff from his pocket and hands it to Roddy. He sniffs it and slips it between his lips. He pats his pockets and sighs.

"It won't light itself," he says to Acne Boy, and the rest of the Horde laugh.

The boy strikes a match against the bark and lights the spliff. Roddy inhales, holds his breath and then blows a cloud of smoke into Acne Boy's face. The Horde laughs again.

Kids aren't allowed to smoke in the Home and, even though Roddy is no respecter of rules, he never risks his skunk stash being seized by the staff.

Jerome's leaf drifts past Roddy and settles on the parched ground. All four of the kids peer up into the tree. Jerome holds his breath. He's sure that they can't see him, but that doesn't mean he isn't afraid. Fear always trumps logic.

Roddy is three years older than Jerome. He's a habitual bully. The King Emperor of the Home and the Horde — Jerome's name for the other kids driven by fear, boredom and joy to serve Roddy's capricious will. He doesn't like people hiding from him. He doesn't like secrets. Discovery would cause brutal punishment. Roddy has promised Jerome a reckoning, a beating. Jerome doesn't know why. Maybe it's his silence or his books that have offended the older boy. Roddy doesn't offer rational reasoning for his acts of violence.

Satisfied that there is nothing of interest hidden in the tree, Roddy takes another pull on his spliff and jerks his head towards the fields beyond the tree. The Horde swaggers away, laughing and swearing at each other.

Jerome takes a deep, shuddering breath. He pulls his phone from his pocket and slips in earbuds. He presses the icon of a radio app. None of the other kids listen to the news. It isn't a cool thing to do.

Unsurprisingly, the ongoing bizarre weather is the dominant story. The newsreader lists yesterday's bewildering, global atmospheric and ecological shifts, followed by a panel of scientists, theologians and conspiracy theorists arguing over a series of explanations.

It's an exponential leap in planetary warming. Chemical weapons leaking into the Earth's atmosphere from a North Korean laboratory. Wind farms have confused the jet stream. It's an alien invasion. It's the Jews. It's the Nazis. It's the Illuminati. It's the end times. He's coming and the number of beast shall be 666. Goddammit, you're all mad, it's just weather and a few animal mutations!

Nobody knows anything. Nobody knows what causes the sudden downpours of rain that are as warm as the Indian Ocean. Nobody knows what was causing the blistering heat that sucks tarmac puddles to the road surface. Or what coaxes muscular weeds, with thick stems and fleshy leaves, into a violent assault on parks and gardens. What type of seeds cause paving stones to crack as they swell. Nobody knows what causes dogs and cats to hide and bark and hiss as if the air causes them pain. Nobody knows why there have been so many miscarriages. Nobody knows where the new insect species have come from or whether they have been there all the time, hiding, waiting. Nobody knows anything, but it doesn't stop people talking as if they do.

Jerome hisses with frustration. There have still been no reports of people experiencing physical changes. Nothing to help make sense of his personal nightmare. Nothing to make him feel less alone.

Careful to maintain his balance, he pulls up his right trouser leg and rolls down a sweaty sock. He counts to five before he can bring himself to look at his ankle. He's still hoping it was nothing but a dream, but when he looks, it's still there. Just above the lateral malleolus, a piece of bone, the length and thickness of two matchsticks placed end-to-end, pokes through his skin and runs through fine hairs flush against his leg.

He'd first dreamt it into existence a week ago. He remembers how the skin had tented with the pressure from below. Then it had split, bloodless and neat, and the pristine bone grew through the wound. His flesh puckered at its base, forming a seal. When he woke, the bone was there, just as he had dreamt it. Last night, the dream came again and the bone started to curl around his calf. When he woke, he found the bone matched the dimensions of his dream.

JEROME COVERS up the bone and looks at his watch. He has to set off for the Home now if he is to be back in time for lunch. So he slips and scrapes his way to the lower branches, dangles and drops to the ground. His landing is poor. He feels his ankle twist; ligaments stretch painfully.

As he makes his way back to The Home, he curses under his breath and tries to cover up his newly-acquired limp.

———————

JEROME MAKES it through lunch without incident. Luckily, Roddy has found another distraction. The Home's King-Emperor drags his chair – legs squealing against linoleum – across the dining room and plonks himself down alongside a girl. He's too close. Invading her personal space. The girl leans away from him, but this just makes him grin and wink back at the appreciate Horde. The girl is quiet and shy. She has wild auburn hair, a spray of freckles across pale cheeks and a face that changes markedly dependent on the angle from which you view it. Sometimes Jerome thinks she's a different person. This makes it difficult for him to remember her name. He knows she hangs around with two other girls, avoiding The Horde. He searches his memory. What's her name? Julie? No, it's Jane. Jane Tully.

Normally Roddy overlooks her, but today, oppressed by the heat and humidity, she's made the mistake of wearing a low-cut vest top that reveals the relative maturity of her body.

She hurries to finish her lunch. Ignores Roddy's attempts at conversation. He switches to crude jokes and looks down the front of her top. He asks her to go down to the fields with him later. She shakes her head and tries to ignore him. He pinches her arm. Tells her not to be a tease.

Jerome can't watch somebody else's torture; his own is enough to bear. He slips from the room and hurries to the sanctuary of his bedroom. Pulling a book from under his mattress, he lies back on his bed. He's reading a natural history manual. Darwin's theories. Nature's numbers. He's soon lost in words and theories. Everybody else will be out in the sunshine this afternoon, so he'll be able to read in peaceful solitude. When the sun angles into his room, he pulls the curtains across. There is no breeze to make them so much as twitch.

After a couple of hours of intensive reading, he becomes sleepy. The air in the room is as hot and heavy as a duvet. He's opened the window, but there's no breeze. Stagnant, hot air. He can hear some kids messing around on the strip of brown grass in front of the Home. From their screams and shouts, he guesses that they're having a water fight. He fantasises about joining in with them – a water fight would be good in this weather – but he knows that he's been a loner for too long now. He can't just walk up and join in. There are rules. Friendship obligations that he just doesn't understand. Gradually, he succumbs to the heat. His eyes close and he drifts away from the yelps and splashes outside.

The dream comes again. This time, he's lying naked on soft soil in the middle of the Forest. Water gurgles nearby. A stream? Birds screech in the air. The bright green canopy above explodes into activity as unseen animals leap from branch to branch. In the distance he hears gentle chimes. Dandelion-like spores drift on a breeze as warm and gentle as a lover's fingers. His body responds to its touch. The spores ride each intake of breath. He sucks them deep into his body. They tickle this throat.

He feels movement on his leg. It's a pleasant, tingling, almost sexual feeling. He looks down. It's the bone. It's growing further from his leg, thickening and twisting clock-wise behind his calf and then back around to his shin. *I like this feeling,* he thinks, and sighs. As if in response, a second bone pierces the skin above his ankle. This one is as fat as his thumb; it twists anti-clockwise around his leg. The bones weave a bone guard around his shin.

There's no pain. Only pleasure. But Jerome knows that this isn't natural. It can't be happening. He's read enough books on the subject. The human body doesn't do this. Fear enters the dream. *I don't want to be a freak.* He concentrates on stopping the bones' growth. To his relief, the dream obeys him.

A new sound enters the dream. It confuses him. It doesn't belong in the Forest. It's an intrusion. The animals hidden in the trees hiss their displeasure. The birds scatter. The noise comes again. A knocking sound. Knuckles on wood. He twists his head but he can see nothing other than bright undergrowth, trees and clouds of spores. Then he hears a voice calling his name. He turns from side to side, but he's alone.

The voice comes louder: *Jerome?* Questioning? Challenging? He realises that the voice is outside the dream and suddenly the spell breaks. His eyes are open and he sits up on his bed, trying to shake the dream out of his head. There are long shadows in his room. The air is still hot. A knock on his door.

"Jerome? Are you in there?" A girl's voice.

Normally, he'd ignore anyone who came to his room. Pretend he wasn't in. But he's still disorientated.

"Yes." His voice is a croak.

"They sent me to fetch you for dinner." He knows the voice, but can't attach it to a name.

Dinner? He's been asleep for hours.

"Tell them... tell them I'm coming," he says.

He can sense her presence outside the door.

"Are you all right?" she asks.

He intends to say that he's fine, but his throat refuses to

cooperate. It's too dry, too full of the memory of the spores. All he can manage is another croak.

The door opens. Jane Tully. He notes that, despite the heat, she's now wearing a baggy sweat-top.

"Are you sure?" She looks genuinely concerned.

Jerome blushes. This is the most attention positive attention any girl at the Home had ever given to him. He feels like he should say something funny, or cool, but knows if he attempts that, his words will just come out gauche or stupid. So he just mumbles that he's fine.

"Let's go, then... before they send the Rottweiler," she says, disappearing into the corridor.

Jerome knows that secretly some kids called Roddy this, but he's surprised to hear Jane say it. She seems too quiet and meek to risk his wrath. Maybe her lunchtime ordeal has emboldened her. He checks his memories; *I know nothing about her*, he thinks. *All I have ever done is look at her across a dining room, tracing the contours of her body with my gaze. I'm as bad as Roddy.*

As he stands to follow her, a searing pain shoots through his right leg from the sole of the foot to the knee. He falls to the floor with a yelp.

Jane dashes back into the room, shutting the door behind her.

"I knew there was something the matter with you," she says. "I could hear you talking in your sleep. Have you got a fever?"

She puts a palm against his forehead. He can smell soap and nicotine. As he pulls her hand away, he sees yellow stains on her fingers. He didn't know that she's a Chimney.

"You're not hot," she says. "Well, no hotter than anybody else. Sit on the bed."

As she helps him up, her body presses against him. He

feels her heat. Sneaks a look at her face. The freckles. Sweat beaded on her top lip. Her eyes are cornflower blue. He winces as pain stabs through his leg again.

"Where does it hurt?" she asks, trying to catch his eye.

"It's my leg, but it's okay now, really."

"Let me have a look at it."

"No." His voice is harsh.

"Don't be stupid. You're in pain," she says, with surprising conviction.

Jane reaches down and takes hold of his right shin. He feels her touch the weave of bones through his jeans and a ripple of pleasure runs through his body. But Jane is pulling her hands away, fingers spread wide. Her shadow-dilated pupils stare at him.

He feels a rising terror. How will she react? Run screaming from the room and bring down the freak-hunting wrath of the Horde? Or show empathy, pity, or even interest? Could the future course of his life be wholly contingent on the reaction of this freckled, teenage girl?

"What's that?" She's whispering.

There is no point in trying to hide the bones. She's felt them. Denial would do nothing except excite further interest or horror. He feels cheated. For the first time, a girl had shown interest in his wellbeing. Now she will discover that he's nothing but a freak.

Carefully, he pulls up the right leg of his jeans. The bones are exactly as he dreamt them. Two of them emerging from neatly puckered holes above the ankle and weaving a protective bone shield around his shin.

Jane stares at the bones. A bead of sweat falls from her nose. She moves a hand towards the bones, then stops. She looks at Jerome, eyes wide.

"Can I touch them?"

Jerome hadn't expected this. He nods.

Gently, as if afraid it might break, she lays a palm against the bone weave. With one finger she traces the flow of bones, inserts her finger into the small gaps left where they criss-cross to see if she can touch the flesh below. She can't.

"Beautiful." It's half a word, half a sigh.

Jerome brushes a trickle of sweat from the side of his face. He does not understand how to respond. He feels a swelling at the crotch and leans forward to hide it.

"What caused it?" she asks.

"I dreamt it."

She looks at him, eyes wide, gauging whether he's lying or joking.

"It's true," he says.

A gruff voice calls up the stairs, telling them both to get down to dinner.

"We have to go," she says, climbing to her feet. "Can you walk?"

The pain in his leg has receded. He nods, but he's still on the bed.

"Will you tell anybody else?" he asks.

Jane turns as she reaches the door. He waits for her answer as the accused awaits the jury's verdict.

She shakes her head.

EVEN THOUGH THE pain in his leg has subsided, Jerome can't eat his dinner. His nerves are alive. He still doesn't know if he can trust Jane. He catches her eye several times during the meal and at one point she's daring enough to smile at him. With a thumping heart, he drops his gaze.

Roddy has seen the smile. From the corner of one eye, Jerome watches him scan the room, calculating the recipient. His gaze comes to rest on Jerome, lingers, and then moves on.

After dinner Jerome dashes through the recreation room before Roddy and the Horde establish camp. He shuts himself in his room and sits cross-legged on his bed, hands tapping against the bone weave, waiting for the deliberate thump of their steps, the door slamming open, the shouts and taunts and the ultimate discovery of his secret.

Nobody comes. Jerome waits for darkness to fall and clambers out of his window into the tropical night air. He creeps through the fringe of shadows around the Home to the hedge that provides a barrier to the fields beyond. Brambles snag his T-shirt as he crouches down and squeezes through a thorny opening. Overripe berries burst against his face. He smells their sickly juice. Thin branches crack underfoot.

"Jerome?" A voice behind him.

He freezes.

"Jerome?"

The voice is more urgent this time.

It's Jane. He can hear her fumbling her way along the hedge towards him. He doesn't know what to do. Why is she out here, following him? He holds his breath. She stumbles and falls and curses.

"Jerome, I know you're you." Now she sounds annoyed.

If he acknowledges her, he knows things could change. He'd be taking the risk that she might become his friend. That she might actually like him. That would complicate things. Make him more vulnerable. He is tired of being alone, but he is scared of opening up to anybody.

He takes a step into the unknown.

"I'm here," he whispers.

A silhouette crawls towards him and for a second he thinks that he's made a mistake, that it isn't Jane, but her freckled face emerges from the shadow. The moon tints her skin platinum.

"Where are you going?"

Jerome pauses for a second; should he tell her about the Tree?

"Follow me," he says.

BY THE TIME they arrive at the Tree, Jane is breathing heavily and they are both slick with sweat. They've waded through three corn fields, crawled under two hedges and climbed over one rusty iron gate to get here. The night does not seem any cooler than the day. The weather forecasters have been promising a storm to clear the air for weeks. It never arrives.

Jerome climbs into the lower branches and hauls a scrambling and huffing Jane after him. Finally, they are sitting amidst the highest branches. They stare out at The Town's flickering lights hanging distant over the blackness of the fields.

"They're like necklaces," says Jane.

Jerome feels a thrill of pride at her appreciation, as if the view is an extension of himself, the strings of light suspended decorously in the air by his hand. This is his secret place. She is the only person with whom he has ever shared it.

Jane uses the bottom of her T-shirt to wipe sweat from her face. Jerome stares at her taut stomach. The shadow of her belly button. The swell of breasts in a white bra. She pulls the T-shirt away from her face, exhaling heavily. Jerome shifts his gaze quickly, feeling himself flush under her knowing gaze.

"Do you like older girls?" she says, laughing.

She's flirting with me, he thinks. *Flirting with me*. His thoughts are spinning, seeking grip, he's Bambi on ice, an explorer in uncharted terrain. Words elude him. He shrugs. She laughs again and licks sweat off her top lip.

Jerome can feel the dream-bones tingling. He wants Jane to touch them again.

"Jerome... can I see the bones again?" she says, and he wonders if she can read his mind.

He nods. Grabs a branch for balance and pulls up his jeans leg to expose the bones. As she traces her fingers over the ivory-coloured weave, he notices for the first time just how precise the patterns and joins are. The absolute precision of nature.

"Did you really dream this?" she asks, still stroking the bones.

He nods, but she isn't looking at him. He realises that he will have to speak.

"Yes," he says, his voice low and husky. "I was in a forest. They just grew."

She strokes his knee and then the bone as if to compare the texture of the two. Jerome sucks in a small breath. Holds it. Bites his lip. An erection pushes uncomfortably against his jeans. Jane smiles and continues her exploration. Her hand is on his thigh.

"It's like something you'd see in a dream, or a film," she says, as if conceding a point to herself. Her voice sounds far away, dreamy. She continues to stroke him.

Jerome's gaze slides over her body. He can't help himself. Tells himself it's okay. She's flirting with him. He imagines her naked. Freckles on her pale breasts. Auburn hair between her legs. Sweat dribbles down his chest. A thick pulse beats in his ear. His breath comes in short bursts. He realises that he's edging towards orgasm. Roughly, he pulls his leg away from Jane. She looks embarrassed, as if she's woken from a trance in which she'd been spilling her darkest secrets.

"We have to get back to the Home," he says. "They'll be checking on us soon."

She nods. He swings his legs down to the lower branches and holds out a steadying hand for Jane. They barely speak on the return journey.

JEROME CAN'T SLEEP. His mind is thick with images of Jane's smiling face, her body, her hands on the bone weave. He masturbated as soon as he was alone, but that hasn't helped. It just cements the images in his mind. He tries counting sheep, but he finds them impossible to focus on. So he shifts to counting the leaves on the Tree. He can see them dangling from slim branches alongside Jane's face. Sleep snatches him.

The Forest hums around him, verdant and ripe. Spores settle onto his face, slowly rolling into the groove of his smile. He feels movement on his left leg. Two bones have emerged from his skin and are twisting their way back and forth, weaving patterns that mirror those on his right leg.

He hears feet padding gently through the undergrowth. He'd prayed for her to come. Jane emerges through a curtain of vines. She's naked and smiling, but her state of undress doesn't excite or even interest Jerome. The rules are different here. The Forest is the home to change. She sits cross-legged at Jerome's feet and smiles at him. Without breaking eye contact, she places her hands on the symmetrical weaves. Jerome knows what he has to do. He knows what she wants. *They're like a necklace*, she said.

He feels energy well up behind his eyes and he concentrates on her neck. A small bulge appears, whiter than the surrounding flesh. The skin splits and puckers, releasing a thin bone.

Jane raises her hands to stroke the bone as it circles her throat. A necklace of bone. A second bone emerges and winds around the first to give the effect more substance. Jane beams. Jerome spreads his arms wide; a magician silently milking the audience's appreciation of an illusion's climax. Jane lies alongside him, in his embrace. He has never felt so happy. The dream blurs to green. He drifts through thoughtless sleep.

***

"YOU FUCKING WEIRDO SPAZ BASTARD!"

Arms slam into Jerome's chest, grabbing the front of his pyjama top. Ripping him from sleep. His vision lags behind the violence. He's in a sweltering hot room. A girl is screaming and crying outside his door. He's dragged from the bed. His head smacks against the floor. Somebody's laughing. Somebody else is kicking him in the stomach. He's coughing and gagging, eyes now open but his vision full of tears.

"Fucker!" Roddy's voice against his ear. "Let's have a look at your zombie legs!"

Somebody wrenches down his pyjama trousers, exposing his genitals and legs. Jerome struggles violently, nearly breaking free of their grip, but then a heavy body lies across him, squeezing all breath from him and preventing any movement. The girl's scream has become sobbing.

Jerome blinks away tears, taking in the scene. Roddy is squatting beside him while one of The Horde lies across him. Half a dozen others crowd around him. Others are squeezing past a body in the doorway to get a look at the torture. Somebody is bouncing up and down on the bed, laughing and clapping.

The body in the doorway is Jane. She's sobbing. Head down. Her hands try to cover the ring of bone around her neck. When she sees Jerome looking at her, she screams at him and disappears into the corridor.

"Shit on a stick!" shouts the boy lying across Jerome.

The Horde has uncovered the bone weaves. Two younger kids scream. One runs from the room. Nobody seems to know what to do next until Roddy raises an arm.

"Freak!" he shouts and drives his fist into Jerome's body. Blows fall on him from every angle. Soon his body is as numb as bone.

He doesn't notice the beating stop. He passes into a state in which any awareness eludes him. When it returns, when he realises that he is Jerome, he is alone in his room. But there is shouting and screaming in the corridor outside. Doors are slamming. A phone rings. The sound of urgent adult voices.

Jerome raises himself onto one arm. Pain surges through his body and it convulses. He gags. Stops moving. Takes deep breaths. When he moves again, he is ready for the pain. But the pain is not the worst sensation. The anger is terrifying. It's burning inside like an uncontrollable wildfire. Consuming everything within the shell of his body. Eating the person who had been Jerome. It scares him, but what can he do? How can he control it? This shitty world will not let him be. He clambers onto his bed and pulls on a pair of tracksuit bottoms.

Outside dawn is spreading a grey light. He opens his window and manoeuvres his battered body through the opening. He flops onto the dead grass outside. His legs aren't working well, but he shuffles his way around the Home to the gap in the hedge. He needs to get to the Tree. He'll be able to think when he gets there. He'll be able to plan.

He stumbles across one cornfield, but the second defeats him. He cannot make it to the Tree. He doesn't have the strength. He's exhausted, and the ridged earth is a trip hazard for every shambolic step he takes. When he falls for the twentieth time, he stays down. He can already feel the sun's blistering heat pressing down on him, and all he has for protection is the corn rising around him.

Thinking of the Tree, he closes his eyes and slips into a state between sleep and unconsciousness. The Tree. The Forest. He needs the Forest. He searches for it. A rising panic grips his unconscious state. He can hear the wind making the Forest's trees creak, he can hear the birds and the chimes, he can feel the humidity and taste the spores, but he just can't open his eyes to see its lush bright green. He can't calm his mind. What if the Horde has damaged his brain with their vicious blows? What if he can never return to the Forest?

The Horde. Everybody in the world is part of the Horde. His mum and dad with their violence and selfishness. The social workers and police. Foster parents and care homes. The Home. Roddy. The Horde is endless and he's been its prey all his life. He needs the Forest to make an end of this vulnerability. He needs to change. Change equals survival.

This sudden certainty relaxes him, and his mind enters the Forest. It spreads about him in its emerald pomp. Jerome claps his hands and laughs, sucking down so many spores that his head hums. He's drunk on spores. Drunk on the possibility of change.

He looks down at his naked legs and watches the bones continuing to weave, climbing higher, fashioning an intricate joint around his knee so that his movement won't be impeded. Other bones are erupting from his skin. From his forearms, his chest, his buttocks, his neck. He even feels bones sprouting from his skull. They pass in front of his eyes, leaving a slit for his vision like a knight's helmet.

During the metamorphosis, he is aware of people outside the Forest, people in the real world passing by, close to his resting place in the cornfield, but they fade and Jerome sinks back into the fullness of his dream.

The bones no longer leave gaps in the weave. Under his direction they form a flawless exoskeleton that is slick, hard and invulnerable. His feet are tipped with long claws and his right hand extrudes a long serrated spike.

Bone encases him.

The transformation has been tiring work. Within his dream, he sleeps and dreams.

THUNDER WAKES HIM. He snaps into a crouch. It's dark and he's surrounded by violently waving corn. The long-promised storm is coming. He stands upright and feels his claws bite into the soil. In the distance, he sees the lights of the Town. Lightning flashes and he glimpses the silhouettes of buildings. More thunder. More lightning, powerful and bright, stabbing down at the buildings. The Town's lights flicker and die. A power cut. He doesn't care. It suits his purpose.

The rain rolls in on the back of violent winds. Spiteful and harsh, it batters corn to the ground; snapping stalks, detaching ears, churning up the soil. The ground is baked hard and can't absorb these sudden volumes. Muddy puddles rise around his feet. The land is choking on the deluge. Mother Nature is waterboarding herself.

Jerome laughs, safe in the sanctuary of his armour. Rain cascades from the bone. He jogs towards the Home.

FLICKERING candles light the interior of the Home. Shadow figures waver on curtains drawn against the storm. A police car is parked on the gravel drive. Nobody is inside it. They are all inside the Home. The Horde is waiting for him. He can visualise them, gathered around Jane, staring at her bone necklace, cursing the monster who conjured it.

Jerome is sure that Jane must hate him, but he can't leave things like this. He has to try to explain to her that desire, not malice or spite, fuelled this act. The world is changing. Maybe he could make her understand.

He twists the handle of the Home's front door. It's locked. He smacks the flat of one hand against the wood, just above the lock, and it flies open. Wind and rain dive into the opening, immediately snuffing out two candles that had been lighting the hallway.

Jerome glimpses an adult standing at the end of the corridor before darkness makes them into a shadow. It looks like a young, uniformed police officer. Jerome moves along the corridor, towards the shadow.

"Who is it?" says the man.

Lightning flashes.

"Christ," says the policeman, turning and scrabbling to open the door behind him.

Jerome is on him in seconds. The police have never helped him. They left him at the mercy of the Horde. The bone spike extending from his right hand skewers the policeman's neck. Hands clutched to the wound, the policeman staggers away from the door, gurgling, stumbling towards the wind and rain, but Jerome takes his bloody neck in both hands and crushes his windpipe. He lowers the body to the floor. He doesn't feel guilty. The Horde is endless and only the strong survive. He knows that now.

He steps over the body and opens the door that the policeman had been guarding. It leads into the wing of The Home that contains the girls' bedrooms . One of the younger girls peeks out from a candlelit room. Jerome growls at her and she shrieks, diving back inside and slamming closed the door.

The door to Jane's room is ajar. He pushes it fully open. Even in the dark, he can sense that it is empty of her belongings. He feels cheated. How dare they deny him the opportunity to explain himself?

Where are they hiding her?

He smashes open bedroom doors, whether or not they are locked. Terrified girls crawl into the corners of their rooms, sobbing, begging the monster to leave them alone. Jerome doesn't touch any of them. He is only interested in Jane. And one other.

He finds Roddy and his three most loyal lieutenants in recreation room. They have lit candles and placed them in each of the pockets of the pool table. When they see Jerome, they raise pool cues as if they are Samurai swords. The only way out of the room is past the monster.

"Jerome?" Roddy's voice is a whisper.

It could be a question, a statement or a plea; maybe it is all of those things. Jerome doesn't really care. He can't be dissuaded from his purpose. He has the implacable resolve of the born-again.

"Where's Jane?" says Jerome.

"Oh, please God, no," says Roddy, dropping his pool cue.

"Jane?" says Jerome.

"They took her... to hospital... please, Jerome..."

Roddy and others back into the corner as Jerome advances on them.

JEROME RAISES his arms to the hammering rain and lets it sluice blood and gore from his body of bone. He didn't linger over the slaughter. He'd no desire to torture Roddy as the boy had tortured him. He simply wanted him dead, removed, relegated to the status of a bad dream.

He realises that he should have asked Roddy *which* hospital Jane was taken to, but he's not too upset with himself. He's still evolving, learning. He has a world to experience anew. And now the reckoning with the Horde has to begin in earnest.

THE EYE & THE ENEMY

I was sitting on the opposite side of the breakfast table to Bo Haskell on the morning he disappeared. One moment he was lifting a fork, balancing a sliver of egg white, moving it slowly towards his mouth, then a look of mild confusion wrinkled his all-American face, and he was gone. His fork clattered onto his plate and the piece of egg slithered off the edge of the table.

A chorus of scraping chairs and yells filled the canteen as my colleagues gathered around his vacant seat. Ruotolo waved his arms through the space like a kid wearing a blind-fold. Dumb fuck. Although I was as shocked as everybody else, I couldn't help thinking it was just typical of Haskell. The grandstanding bastard had to be first in everything.

The blare of a klaxon filled the building and a loud-speaker ordered everybody back to their quarters. In my room, I lowered my bulk onto my bed and let a broad smile crease my face. I giggled. I clamped a hand over my mouth to contain my laughter. Haskell had gone. No need to send that letter to Santa Claus. I would be Number One again.

My heart lurched the second after the guard closed my

door and a bolt clunked into place. Confusion replaced elation. I didn't know the doors *had* outside locks. My protruding belly pressed against the door as I yanked on the handle. It was secure. I could hear the steady squeak of boots retreating down the corridor. They couldn't do this to me. I was shaking as I thumped the palm of my hand against the wood.

"Open this door now."

Silence.

"What the hell do you think you're doing? You can't do this."

More silence.

"I want to see the Director. I demand to see Director Macintosh."

Nearby, one of my colleagues was banging against his door. Even though his voice was muffled, I could tell he was afraid.

I DIDN'T WANT to join the army to fight the Communists. I didn't care about them or Cuba. I just thought it'd be cool to get my hands on some serious artillery. To find some power. Some respect. But it was destined not to be; I had a sleepy thyroid gland that numerous doctors had failed to wake, and twenty stones of blubber on a five-foot-ten frame is not an ideal fighting chassis.

The offer from the Institute was the defining moment in my life. I'd always suspected that I had some psychic ability. As a kid, I always won when we played hide and seek because I just *knew* where people were hiding. I *knew* what pie my mother had baked before its smell reached me on the back porch. But it was an incident at a county fair, documented in the local paper, that drew the attention of the Institute. I correctly predicted the winning number on a Wheel of Fortune – a one in fifty chance – ten consecutive times. I thought this might earn me some respect, but people just called me a freak.

The Institute took a different view. Men in smart suits came to our house and offered me the chance to join a government institution researching the feasibility of using psychic abilities in the war against communism. I was eighteen years old. They talked to me alone. Man to man. If I accepted, my parents could not be told the specifics of my work. I nearly leapt out of my seat and kissed them. I said goodbye to my family that evening.

I started on the Institute's training programme with three new recruits. We practised *seeing* symbols on cards sealed in envelopes. It was child's play. I blew the others out of the water with my success rate. Immediately, I was moved onto the Remote Scanners Programme and given a cocktail of drugs to enhance my abilities. The remote scanners were the elite psychics. Working from empty rooms nicknamed *prayer cells*, the scanners would try to *see* military installations, troop manoeuvres and research centres that thousands of miles away.

At the end of the first month, I *saw* a missile silo in the Ukraine that the others had unsuccessfully sought for over a year. The image was so clear I could read notes a guard was scribbling on his clipboard. That's when everybody started to call me *The Eye*.

"I APOLOGISE FOR THE LOCKDOWN," said Director Macintosh, sitting on my desk chair. "But it's a necessary precaution. We can't take any chances. The rest of the programme is too precious."

"It was just a little unexpected," I said.

"I understand your concerns," said the Director, raising his hands, palms towards me. Against my better judgment, I found myself calmed by the gesture. He radiated an aura of such benign authority the other scanners secretly nicknamed him *God*. That fitted with my view of him – all myth and no trousers.

"Lack of information makes me jittery. And if I'm jittery, I can't scan," I said.

"Of course," said the Director. "You're our number one scanner. We will need you in A1 shape to help us find out what happened to Bo."

I let his words fan the embers of my ego before wondering whether he would consider me top dog if Bo Haskell *hadn't* disappeared. The Director stood and made his way to the door. His step didn't seem as sprightly as usual. Maybe even God was prone to tension.

"What was Bo working on?" I asked.

The Director took a deep breath and met my gaze. "I can't reveal the exact details of his project yet, but he was using very powerful new stimulants. Very pure."

"What was he scanning for?"

"The enemy. As always." The Director smiled. "I won't lock your door anymore."

I COULDN'T SETTLE to anything constructive for the rest of the day. I was too agitated by what The Director had told me. *Very powerful new drugs.* I used to alpha-test all the new drugs. Me. *The Eye.*

I remembered the day Haskell sauntered into the Institute, a blandly handsome, white-toothed paragon of charm. He was a natural actor and he knew how to push people's buttons. Within a month, he had God and the rest of the Institute in the palm of his hand. I was the only one who saw the glimmer of ego in his eyes.

I looked out my window at the flat, moonlit vista beyond the barbed-wire fence that ran around the compound. Jesus, Texas was boring. They said the desolate landscape aided scanning.

I glimpsed myself mirrored in the window. My torso was a huge bell of flesh obscuring the waistband of my shorts. My breasts would have looked good on a Hollywood starlet. I squeezed them and pouted at myself. At least the forest of my beard partially obscured my increasing collection of chins. Disgusting. I focused beyond my reflection, looking deeper into my room. Bo Haskell was sitting on my bed.

"Don't stop, I was just getting horny," he said.

"Jesus H. Christ," I said, spinning. Goosebumps needled my flesh and my heart laboured into action. "You're back."

"Not really." He shook his head. He was looking disdainfully at my fat belly, and so I tugged a T-shirt over my head. I was burning with embarrassment and hate.

"What do you mean?"

"I won't be able to keep myself here for long. I can already feel it pulling me back. Nobody else can see me. Naturally, I tried to speak to everybody else before coming to you. But you're the only one with enough of an ability."

"You know how to make a girl feel wanted." I was regaining my composure now. Evaluating this bizarre situation.

"You'd do the same."

"Probably." I noticed smudges of dirt on his cheeks. His hands and clothes were similarly stained. "What happened to you in the canteen?" I asked. "Showboating as usual?"

"Ha, showboating." He shook his head again and looked at the floor. A sudden surge of elation ran through my body. He was worried. The great Bo Haskell was worried.

"I've been taking a new enhancement drug, Jacob 3. After the last dose I experienced a buildup of a... pulling sensation within me. It's hard to explain. It's as if I was being dragged towards a magnet that attracted flesh. As if molecules within me were displacing. Yesterday morning the pull was so strong that I just... went." He clicked his fingers.

"Where to?"

"I don't know. Probably the Soviet Union. But God knows where, precisely. All I've found so far is... I don't know what to call them... slag heaps, as far as the eye can see."

"A nuclear testing ground?"

"Maybe," he said uncertainly. He stared at the floor again and hesitated. "Eye, I don't know how to control this. I don't even know if I'll be able to come back again."

Suddenly he stopped and looked around himself anxiously. He spoke quickly. "I can feel it starting again. Listen to me. Be my link to the Director. I know you hate me, but we have to work together on this. Okay?"

"Sure," I said, smiling reassuringly. I tried not to lick my lips.

He clutched his sides and grimaced. "I can't stay here anymore. It's too difficult."

He disappeared.

There was a smear of ash on my bedclothes. I beat at it with my hand until there was nothing left.

DIRECTOR MACINTOSH STOOD ramrod-straight before the assembled scanners. I was in the front row.

"Although we are not giving up hope of locating Bo Haskell, it has been a week, and we have received no contact from him. It saddens us deeply. The President himself has asked to be kept aware of Bo's status. However, the project Bo was working on must continue. Normally, we wouldn't ask for a volunteer; we'd designate a replacement. The Institute is not a democracy. However, you all witnessed what happened to Bo. Therefore, *I am* appealing for volunteers."

I raised my hand.

I was the only volunteer.

Director Macintosh smiled. "I was hoping we could rely on the Eye."

I signed the consent papers in the Director's office. He shook my hand vigorously. "You're going to be famous, Eye."

Fuck you and your megawatt smile, Bo Haskell.

In the surgery, Dr Hinckle gave me my first shot of the new drug. It glowed like sunlit amber in the syringe and filled my arm with a warm tingling sensation. He dabbed cotton wool on the pinprick needle mark and then scribbled notes on a chart. "Same time tomorrow," he said.

AS PART of the Jacob 3 monitoring process, I moved from my quarters to Observation Room 1, which some scanners called the Confessional. Stupid name, if you asked me. I kept to the official acronym: OR1. They furnished it just like every other room, but it had a one-way mirror covering the entirety of one wall and a camera perched high in the corner. Occasionally a disembodied voice would ask me questions or offer reassurance from a hidden speaker.

On my first night in OR1, Bo Haskell came back again. I was sitting on my bed reading. Suddenly he was there, leaning on the end of my bed, bent double, gasping for air. A thick layer of ash covered him. His eyes were red and watering, leaving streaks down his cheeks.

"You've got to help, Eye." His voice gurgled as if his lungs were full of molten tar. "Did you speak to the Director?"

Shit. I looked at the one-way mirror.

"Eye? Did you speak to the Director?"

"Hang in there, Bo. We're doing everything we can to bring you back," I said, laying on my most sincere tone.

A voice I had never heard crackled over the loud-speaker. "Are you seeing something, Eye?"

"I'm seeing Bo."

I heard the camera whine as it panned around the room. They couldn't see or hear him. Thank God.

"I don't know where they sent me," he said, "but it's killing me. There's a mist made of grit and I can't stop breathing it in." A coughing fit doubled him over and he hawked a ball of gritty black spittle onto the floor as if to prove his point.

"We're doing everything we can, Bo."

"I know, I know," he said. He sat on the end of my bed, bent over and wheezing. I was shocked by how feeble he looked. There were sores on his arms and neck. "If that place is in the Soviet Union, then they're welcome to it. It makes Pittsburgh look like Malibu." He laughed weakly and spat out more midnight-hued phlegm.

The pinprick in my arm tingled. Where had they sent him?

"Ask him if he has seen a city," said the loudspeaker.

Bo looked up. "Yeah. Tell them I saw a city in the distance, just before I was yanked back here. It was in the middle of a vast plain. Some massive, industrial hellhole, covered in smoke. It looks Soviet. I could see fire coming out of massive chimneys. I think there are planes or maybe airships circling above it."

I looked at the one-way mirror. "He says he saw a city just before he was pulled back here."

The loudspeaker was silent.

"Ask them what city it is," said Haskell.

"He wants to know what city it is," I said to my reflection.

Nothing from the loudspeaker.

"I'm fucking taking a fall for them. Why won't they tell me?" There was desperation and fear in his voice. For a second, I felt sorry for the arrogant bastard.

"Can you tell Bo what the city is?" I asked again. And again, nobody answered.

Haskell was on his feet, striding towards the mirror. He didn't cast a reflection. When he slapped his palms against the glass, they made no sound.

"Why won't they tell me?"

I shook my head. "Don't worry, I'll find out before I come."

"What?"

"I'm the new alpha tester." It sent a thrill through me to see his face when I said this.

"Don't do it, Eye. You've seen what's happening to me." He ran across the room and leant over me. I backed away from him until I was horizontal on my bed. I could see how deeply the filth was ingrained in the flesh around his blood-shot eyes. His lungs wheezed and popped. His sores wept sticky fluid. "Don't let them do *this* to you."

He vanished, leaving a fine shower of ash to fall on me.

"Are you still seeing Bo?" asked the disembodied voice.

I didn't answer them.

"ROLL UP YOUR SLEEVE PLEASE," said Dr Hinckle.

My body felt heavier than ever before. I hadn't slept the previous night. I kept seeing Haskell's bloodshot eyes and hearing the asthmatic symphony of his lungs.

"Could you please roll up your sleeve," said the doctor, sounding tired and nervous. He shook his head and tutted as he pushed more of the amber fluid into my veins.

"Where did they send Bo Haskell, Doctor?"

"I'm just the physician. Don't ask me." His hands were shaking as he withdrew the needle. A bead of blood welled around the puncture mark. Somehow the syringe slipped from his fingers and the needle embedded itself in the leather of his shoes. Hopping comically, he pulled it out and yanked off his shoe.

"You signed the papers. It's too late to ask questions now," he said, inspecting his foot for any signs of a puncture mark.

As guards escorted me back to the observation room, I saw two people cut across the corridor. They were maybe a hundred feet away from me. Director Macintosh was one of the group. At first I thought the other was a woman wearing a long dress. Then he turned and faced me. A neat grey beard covered his face. He disappeared down another corridor with the Director before I could take a closer look at him.

LATER THAT DAY, I asked to speak to Director Macintosh. Over the speaker, a voice told me he was not available and then refused to give a time when he would be free. I told them that this wasn't how I expected an alpha-tester to be treated. The voice said it would pass my sentiments to the Director.

I shuffled around my room, trying to occupy myself with books or my journal, but I couldn't settle to anything. How could they treat me like this? I was the one with the ability and yet they were expecting me to behave like a lab rat. I sat on my bed and stared at the door. I hoped they wouldn't have the audacity to lock it again. I heard footsteps pass outside the room. Voices muttering, then fading. Who were the men I'd seen with the Director?

The isolation and silence gnawed at me. My memory kept conjuring up the sound of Haskell's laboured breathing.

Don't let them do this to you.

I paced, stamping loudly to block out the memory of his voice. Eventually I came to a halt standing in front of the door.

"Is this door locked?" I asked. Behind me, I heard the whirr of the camera.

No answer.

I placed my hand on the handle.

"I said, is this door locked?"

"Please step away from the door," said the voice through the speaker.

"Is it locked?"

"Please stand back from the door."

I turned the handle. The door was locked. I rattled it and then threw my bulk impotently against the wood.

"I want to talk to the Director now," I demanded, striding towards the mirror. "I do not expect to be treated like an animal."

"The Director is not available at the moment."

"When will he be available?"

"I'm not able to say."

"Who are you? I don't know your voice. I want your name so that I can report your uncooperative behaviour to the Director when I see him."

The speaker buzzed with static, nothing else.

"Give me your name, fucker!" I shouted with my face an inch away from the mirror.

There was no response. I spun around in a rage and saw Bo, lying on the floor on the opposite side of my room, gasping for air, trying to push himself upright. He was black with ash and his shirt had been ripped away, revealing bloody gashes across his chest. His hair was smoking and one side of his face had been badly burnt. Patches of red raw skin were visible through the crisp black surface. Small flames danced on one trouser leg.

"Oh my God." I grabbed a sheet from the bed and threw it over him to douse the flames. The sheet passed through him and settled on the floor. It looked as if he was lying on the sheet.

He opened his mouth but couldn't speak. His lungs

were wheezing like punctured bellows. As he struggled to form words, the burnt skin on his face cracked to reveal more raw flesh beneath. "—had to warn you."

"What are you seeing, Eye?" said the speaker voice.

I ignored it and spoke to Haskell. "Warn me about what?"

"Jacob 3..."

"What about it?"

"The enemy."

"Yes."

"Devil... sent me to Hell."

"What?"

The disembodied voice, urgent: "Please tell us what you are seeing, Eye."

"Fuck you," I said, turning to the mirror. When I looked back, Bo had vanished again.

The Devil. Hell.

"I want to speak to the Director now." I spoke each word slowly, fiercely.

"The Director..."

I cut the voice off before it could finish. "Is not available. I know. Well, I am and I want to see him now."

Static crackled from the speaker. Then silence.

My panic left me no other option than to break the Institute's cardinal rule. I scanned within the perimeter. It was wonderfully easy and empowering. I closed my eyes and visualised the room I was in. I walked out into the corridor, drifting along its length until I reached the door that led into the observation control room, and I pushed with my mind. I'd never been into the room, but its image flooded my thoughts.

Director Macintosh was standing at the mirror, watching me. On one side of him stood the man I had seen

in the corridor. He was wearing a priest's robe, not a dress..
In the corner of the room, Ruotolo sat on a chair. Even
before he spoke I knew he had sensed me.

"He's scanning us," said Ruotolo.

"What?" said Director Macintosh.

"He's definitely in the room."

The Director grabbed the microphone. "Eye, you know
it is *strictly* against Institute protocol to scan within the
perimeter."

The priest spoke. His voice was calm and certain. He
smiled. "Macintosh, I don't think we should continue with
this charade. The Lord's will must be done. We all know
this. And it's necessary that some of his foot soldiers must
perish and become martyrs."

The Director's shoulders slumped. He spoke into a
walkie-talkie. "Instigate restraint code red. Doctor Hinckle
to OR 1. Jacob 3, I repeat, Jacob 3."

I watched through the one-way mirror as my body was
manhandled onto a trolley and tied down by four guards.
Doctor Hinckle appeared and pushed more amber fluid into
my body. Suddenly, I was back in my body, looking up at
the guards' faces which hovered blurrily above me.

"It's a booster," said Doctor Hinckle, as his face swam
into view.

Immediately, I experienced the dizzying, pulling sensation that Haskell had found so difficult to explain.

The priest's face loomed into view. "God's righteous
sword will protect you, son."

Director Macintosh: "Your country is proud of you."

"I will fuck you all," I said.

Then I left that place.

THE SKY WAS CHARCOAL. Grey ash around my feet. Rivers of lava ran across the vast plain towards a city that defied description. A towering, black monstrosity crowned with fire. A thousand roads led towards it, each paved with shapes that, as soon as I started to walk, revealed themselves to be the faces of the dead, their lips sewed shut, eyes swiveling, skin filthy, ripped and offering glimpses of bone. Great shapes wheeled above the city. One turned and winged its way towards me. I felt absurdly calm and unbearably excited. The desire to see what nightmare sat in the black heart of the city seized me. I reached out, stepping away from my body, rushing across the plain, through the shadow of the approaching beasts, and into the city. A multitude of terrifying sights assailed me but I did not close my senses to them – giant spiders crafted from a dozen people stitched together the beasts' eyes fashioned from clusters of heads; crowds of flayed bodies, red an oozing, lashing each other with barbed whips, babies in barrels of ash, blood and bone and burning. I flew onwards.

Finally, I came to a huge plaza. The Devil was waiting for me there, and he laughed at my audacity. Stepping towards me, he smiled. Held out his hand. When I kissed his fingers, fire filled my mouth. I did not cry out. He told me he could find much work for me to do. I realised then what I had been looking for all my life.

ABOUT THE AUTHOR

Simon Paul Woodward is the author of the **Deathlings Chronicles** series and **Dead Weapons**. He makes his online home at www.simonpaulwoodward.com.

You can connect with Simon on Facebook at www.facebook.com/simonpaulwoodwardauthor.

and send him an e-mail at simonpaulwoodward@icloud.com if the mood strikes you.

ALSO BY SIMON PAUL WOODWARD

ALL THE DEAD THINGS

Deathlings Chronicles Book 1

A boy on the run. A dead girl leading a rebellion. Time is running out to save the world of the living.

The deathlings believe Stan is the Seer, a human destined to be their doom. They'll stop at nothing in their pursuit of him, even breaking time itself. Now Stan must find his way to the truth, before the deathlings steal his soul. If he fails, they'll destroy the balance between the worlds of the living and the dead forever.

ALL THE DEAD SEAS

Deathlings Chronicles Book 2

Pirates rising from the grave. A Cornish village that may not survive the night. A boy fighting to save his dead sister's soul.

Tom blames himself for his sister's death. When he returns to Little Sickle, the village where she died, he's shocked to learn that her soul is still imprisoned there. Now he has one night to face his guilt, uncover the village's wicked past and rescue her from a crew of bloodthirsty, deathling pirates. Damnation or redemption will be his by dawn.

ALSO BY SIMON PAUL WOODWARD

DEAD WEAPONS

A standalone YA Science-Fiction Thriller

A young man framed for murder. Cyborg black-ops soldiers. A race to save a missing father.

Ciaran agrees to do one last job for this gangster brother. Delivering an AI-powered gun, stolen from a covert government agency, to an underworld boss. As payment, he learns that their soldier father's death was faked. When the job goes wrong, he's framed for murder and forced to flee the police, gangsters and cyborg black-ops soldiers. As his pursuers close in, Ciaran discovers a link between his father's disappearance and the covert agency. Now it's a race against time to stop their plans and save his father from a fate far worse than death.

First published in Great Britain, the USA and Europe by
musingMonster Books, London in October 2020.

www.simonpaulwoodward.com

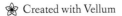 Created with Vellum

ACKNOWLEDGMENTS

Some of these short stories are brand new, a couple were written a number of years ago, and one goes back to my formative writing years, meaning any truly representative list of acknowledgements would need to be exceptionally long. So, I will kick off with a general thank you to all the friends, family and fellow writers who have supported, encouraged and occasionally told me to *have a word with myself* me over the years. You know who you are and your support means the world.

Specific thanks for this book go to my brilliant editor Tim Major who ruthlessly corrected and polished the text and Stuart Bache for the stunning cover design.

As always, huge love and thanks to my wife, Tracy, for being there for me.

www.simonpaulwoodward.com

Printed in Great Britain
by Amazon